Cover Design © 2021 by Ariel Curit
Cover Art © 2021 by Chester Ainsley

Dedicated to my best friend Evie

The person who read almost all of the drafts of Lost Faith.

TUMBLING STONES PACK

alphas ;;

singing crow ... large smokey gray female Cane Corso with scars littering her chest.

scrawny raven ... midnight black female Doberman Pinscher with narrowed brown eyes.

council members ;;

rippling river ... large chocolate brown male Newfoundland with dark brown eyes.

drowning shrew ... snowy white male saluki with cream colored markings.

gray wind ... gray and white female Keeshond with fluffy chest fur.

poisoned rowan ... pitch black female Saluki with chestnut eyes.

heir ;;

birch ... brindle male Doberman Pinscher mix with beautiful white eyes.

shamans ;;

cleared sky ... stormy gray Blue Lacy female with a white patch on her chest.

jagged paw ... long-furred ebony black
male mutt with a twisted paw.

guards ;;

kit ... fluffy black and brown male German Shepherd.

rushing cascade ... small amber-colored female
Boykin Spaniel mix.

drizzled olives ... black, brown, and white female
Boxer with chestnut brown eyes.

red fang ... small red and white male Bull Terrier.

muddy ears ... white female Pitbull with brown ears.

loud tail ... large male Sararbi Dog with a tan pelt.

hunters ;;

melting ice ... light gray and white female Siberian
Husky with honey colored eyes.

cracked twig ... black and white male Cardigan Welsh Corgi.

timid fawn ... white female Greyhound with brindle patches.

buzzing firefly ... tricolor female chihuahua with long fur.

swishing fern ... black, brown, and white, American Foxhound.

rookies ;;

creek ... dark ginger male Golden Retriever
with dark brown eyes.

willow ... creamy colored female Golden Retriever.

hollow ... black, tan, and white female Sheltie.

dams ;;

flowering tulips ... small tan and white Pembroke

Welsh Corgi with a pink flower crown.

squawking parrot . . . black female Puli with dark brown eyes.

pups ;;

bear . . . tan male Corgi mix with black mixed into his fur.

chase . . . brindle and white male Corgi Mix.

pigeon . . . tan and black female Belgian Malinois.

storytellers ;;

cinnamon . . . blue merle female Australian Shepherd
with a red bandana.

chased turkeys . . . silver male Irish Wolfhound
with scars scattered around his snout.

short aspen . . . brown male Chinese Crested
Dog with lighter markings.

PROLOGUE

Her paws pounded against the shivering cobblestone path while her gaze darted around. Snow was piling up against buildings while chatter danced around. The breath slowly escaped her, turning into fog as it did. Tail swaying back and forth slowly, nearing an alleyway.

"Was this really a great idea," She mumbled. The Golden Retriever looked up at the sky, darkness swallowing her whole. Her tail was slowing down as each second went by. She shook her head softly, waves drowning in her eyes.

She was young, yet she had made many mistakes. "It probably wasn't," She murmured, her voice inaudible to those who slid in the shadows. Her paws shuffled as they slammed into the snow.

The female plopped her belly down into the bone-chilling snow letting the cold take over. Her ears soon pinned back, chaining themselves down. Paws scratching at her snout as she let the overwhelming thoughts race around her head.

"What are you doing, youngling?" A deep voice questioned. It was a dark tan French Mastiff, he wore many scars on his pelt. He also wore many collars that covered some of the scars. The most noticeable scar that he had was over his eye, the one that was tightly shut.

The female let her paws go limp and glanced back at the male that had approached her. "What do you want?" She asked, no emotion clinging to her voice. Her honey-colored eyes were wary as they were fixed onto the male.

"Well, I don't want anything but I can take you in," He murmured. "Away from the cold." The male added, taking a step back.

Her head tilted to the side and her eyes narrowed. "What for?" She knew he wanted something from her. Everyone wanted something in this village. The female climbed to her paws, now sitting.

"Maybe, a little information about your pack,"

"*Former pack,*" She growled. Her tail whipping back and forth as she glared at him. Her floppy ears were pinned back against her delicate skull. The female's eyes turned into slits as she stared at the older canine.

"Yes, your former pack." The male growled, his eyes resting on the female. "Do we have a deal?"

CHAPTER ONE

He lowered his belly to the ground, leaning his chest forward. The smell of rabbit danced around his delicate nose. The male would be able to catch the rabbit. He was fast enough and strong enough, *hopefully*. He would just have to get his timing perfect. The male was good enough to hunt prey, having most of the traits he would need, but he wasn't the smartest. Although, even with his flaws he was training to be a hunter.

The male's ginger haunches wiggled as he continued to stalk forward. The rabbit wasn't in sight but he could smell it: His tail swayed back and forth as anxiety crawled into him. He knew he was being watched, they were testing all of the rookies today. What scared him the most though was that the alphas could be watching.

The scent came closer with each step he took. He was careful for the most part not to rub his leg on a shrub on accident. Any sudden noise would be able to scare off his potential catch.

His ears flicked to the side as he heard the smallest crunch of a leaf. They were near. They were watching him. He rolled his shoulders before continuing to stalk the scent.

A flash of creamy brown fur met his eye. It was the rabbit! He could finally see it. Now he just needed to hunt it. It should be fairly easy or so, he thought.

He wiggled his haunches as he watched the rabbit nibble on some berries near a bush. Their large ears flicked while they became wary of their surroundings. The mammal didn't notice him yet, but it would in a matter of time.

The Golden Retriever needed to take his chance, but he

didn't. Then again, he wasn't the smartest with hunting, especially with rabbits. He didn't know how to hunt them even though the older dogs tried to teach him almost everyday, but everytime he didn't do it correctly.

He wiggled his haunches and leaped forward, lips curled back in a snarl. His fangs shimmered as the sunlight poured down onto him.

The rabbit's head whipped around, alert. It quickly turned his head around, staring at the large male. Within seconds it turned and sprinted off, before Creek could even move a paw.

"Moose Scraps!" He cursed, whipping his head around. His tail was raised as he let his glare explore the shrubs that surrounded him. Large redwood trees filled the grounds, growing taller everyday. The trees were a dark red color with moss climbing up them.

A new scent reached his ebony colored nose, twitching. It smelled like raspberries and peppermint mixed together. It was a weird combination but it smelt nice. His eyes soon widened and a whimper soon escaped him as he realized who it was. "I uh, uhm, sorry for not catching the rabbit, Mrs. Crow."

"It's fine, young one," She murmured. Her tail was swaying back and forth as she gazed down at the smaller canine. The female's nose twitched as a droplet fell on it, making itself at home. Her dark colored eyes were soft unlike her posture.

He threw his gaze down at his paws, not wanting to look his alpha in the eye. "Are-are you sure?" The male questioned. His paws shuffled around, mud fighting to get their way in between his paws. His ears flicked as he felt her eyes clawing at his fur.

"I am sure, *Creek*." She barked, raising her head. A small smirk danced onto her face and she lifted his head up with one of her front paws. Mud leaving their mark on the bottom of his snout.

He backed up, stumbling on a small twig. The alphas usually didn't bother saying the names of pups or the names of rookies, since they didn't have *proper* names. "Oh, uh okay..." Creek mumbled. He didn't dare move. He didn't want to disrespect Singing Crow in any way.

"You should get back to hunting." She suggested, flicking her tail. "Also, don't tell anyone about this. I wasn't supposed to be here." She whispered, a small chuckle fighting its way out of her.

He nodded, not letting a single word out of him. Creek whipped around, running, not looking back. The trees were blurs as he ran, paws pounding down against twigs and dead leaves. This was an amazing way to scare away prey yet he continued to do it anyways.

The male raised his snout, taking in the scents that danced around the forest. There was a faint smell of a family of squirrels, they should still be near but he wouldn't want to risk it. Scents of mice were the strongest. There must have been a nest of them somewhere. If there was, he could easily catch most of them. Not all of them. There was a rule that the pack had, *don't hunt all because if we hunt all, there will be none.*

He shoved his nose to the ground, following the trail that the scent had made. Paws went silent as he lowered his belly. Creek had to be careful. Mice were one of the hardest animals to hunt. They could hear someone's paws from miles away or well that's what everyone was told.

The scent grew stronger as his pace went faster. In a matter of seconds, his nose hit a tree stump where the scent was strongest. There was a small hole in the large tree, he wouldn't be able to fit his paw in it but he could for sure, put one of his claws in there. Hunting mice was a two dog job but he was positive he would be able to catch at least three of them, on his own.

He lifted his snout into the air, a small almost silent howl escaping him, dancing in the air. Mice soon scattered around, escaping their burrow that he had dug his claw into. *Moose Scraps! They have an exit to their little house! I'm so stupid! Ugh.* The thoughts raced around his head as he circled the tree, trying to catch an eye of one of those little bastards.

Creek managed to find a blur of gray fur. Licking his chops, he wiggled his haunches and pounced where the mouse was running. Paws on its back, weighing it down. He brought his snout down to where its neck was, fangs hovering above the neck. Creek made the killing bite to its neck, fast and easy, not wanting to cause pain to the animal.

"Thank you for this prey," He mumbled, bringing his gaze up to the sky. The male picked up the prey he had caught and started to walk in the direction that camp was placed.

The hunters wouldn't be too impressed but he had tried. Maybe they would make him into a guard! A whimper rippled in his throat as the thought came to mind. They wouldn't. They couldn't. He would be a terrible guard.

"They'll be happy that i managed to catch one prey! One prey might not be a lot but it's still prey in the end," He mumbled, his voice muffled. "Right?"

The scent of *honey* came to his nose this time, none of his packmates usually smelt like that. His head tilted to the side and his brow furrowed. Creek's long tail raised, lips curling back in a snarl. "Who are you?" He called out, his voice continued to be muffled.

"I am bumble, a seller that travels the world!" A sweet voice barked, revealing stormy gray fur. She was much taller than Creek, collars lining her neck. Her tail was swaying back and forth while the glasses that were in their own little pouches made noises as they touched each other.

He rolled his eyes, "Listen, *Bumble*, we don't want little village dogs in our pack." Creek growled, his floppy ears pressing against his fragile skull. His tail continued to be raised, showing the female in front of him that he was in charge.

Bumble furrowed her brow, her green eyes shimmering. "Well, that isn't a nice way to greet a visitor." She murmured, tail continuing to sway back and forth. The female shot a cautious glance over to her glasses of jam. "I am not a village dog and I was invited here by..." Her voice trailed off, trying to think of the name. "*Scrawny Raven* and *Singing Crow* invited me here,"

11

She murmured.

"O-oh," He mumbled, dipping his head. "I'm sorry, the name's Creek. I can bring you to the camp," Creek offered. A small forced smile made its way on his face as he gazed at the female. Why would they let a pampered mutt into the pack? Especially one of those annoying travellers.

"That will be great," She murmured. "Would you like some jam in return?" Bumble questioned, her head tilting to the side. The tip of her tail had a small scar wrapping around it, along with loss of fur. It was probably from getting her tail stuck when she was making jam.

His nose scrunched up in disgust. "Uh, no thank you," He mumbled. Paws crunched down on leaves and twigs, scaring the prey that were stalking them. "What do they taste like though...?" Creek questioned, not being able to fight the curiosity that was blazing through him.

"Well, I brought mango jam, pear jam, and some apple jam! So they kind of taste like that and of course I added my secret ingredient!" She barked, a smile splattered on her face, a masterpiece. Her paws were delicate, not touching the obstacles that littered the forest floor, more silent than a mouse. "Apple jam is my personal favorite," Bumbled added.

"I've never tried mango or pear." He barked, his head tilted to the side. "I've tried apple before, but I was a pup then so I don't remember what it tastes like." The rookie barked, his tail giving the small swish to the side while his heart fluttered.

"Well, mango and pear are really good, they have a very sweet taste." She explained, lifting up one of her paws as she spoke.

He tilted his head to the other side this time. "What do they look like? I know apples are big and red but I don't know about these other strange fruits." Creek barked, slowing his pace. The sunlight fought with the trees wanting to slow dance on their backs.

"Mangos can be a mixture of many colors, like uhm yellow, green, and a beautiful pinkish red." She explained,

12

matching her pace with the male who was walking beside her. She opened her maw again to speak, but Creek interrupted her.

"Are pears yellow too? The jam looks yellow," He pointed out, tilting his head back to the other side this time. His tail was swaying back and forth, yet faster and not forced this time around.

She shook her head softly, "They are actually green!" Bumble barked, a tiny giggle escaping her. She furrowed her brow as the male glanced down at her jam. "Would you like some now?" The female questioned.

"Like your collar?" He asked, pointing out her cacti green collar, it looked well made too. Completely, oblivious to her question, only focused on what the fruits looked like.

"Uh, no, much lighter actually." She explained, letting her gaze explore her surroundings. It was like nothing she's seen before. The Weimener has been to many beaches, forests, mountains, but never a forest like this. The trees looked as if they went on forever, reaching the end of the sky.

He nodded, "Oh, okay," Creek mumbled. What she said was so intriguing to him and he didn't know why. His tail continued to swish back and forth, pounding against the wind that fought with him. "I think I heard one of the storytellers saying they were rounded shaped," He added.

"They kinda are rounded shaped, now that I think about it." She murmured, her paw making a small thud when the ground dropped by a few inches. Her tail flicked to the side as she let out a small stunning hum. "How far are we from your camp?" Bumble asked, her eyes darting around.

"Not too far!" He barked, beginning to dance around. "I'm sure you'll love it there, I promise." At first he wasn't so sure, but she turned out to be a pretty cool dog. Well, at least for now she was.

Cries ran through the air and dogs hid their pups. Blood was traced around the camp, from the entrance to the middle. There lay a deceased dog with wounds throughout their body.

They were so severe to the point that no sane dog would do this.

"Wha-what happened?" Creek shrieked, his eyes wide in terror. His paws stumbled back as disbelief circled his eyes like a swarm of angry bees. The male's tail was stuck in behind his quivering legs.

An Australian Shepherd whipped around, "He's dead, *rookie!*" She snarled, her eyes closed. "Or do you need your eyesight checked, mutt?" Her nose twitched as her claws dug into the soil. The female's snowy white ears pressed back against her head as she glared at Creek.

A howl broke out into the air, eyes squeezed shut. "We mustn't argue with a dead one among us," She howled, her pelt a beautiful midnight black. Her thin-furred tail was raised, ready to slap anyone with it, if someone snapped back at her. She wasn't to be argued too. She was one of the alphas.

Her mate stood by and gave a stiff nod. She left blue paw prints behind her; dipping her head she told her mate it was time.

Scrawny Raven stepped forward to the body, sinking her teeth into the small canine's scruff.

He closed his eyes, not wanting to watch the ceremony. The male cared for this male but he wasn't his favorite, he was always snapping at him when he was alive. Even though he was in shock for the dead body, he didn't care for the canine passing.

CHAPTER TWO

Bumble watched as Creek glanced over at the storyteller then at the body, the process repeated. Her paws shuffled in the dirt as she avoided contact of cautious dogs who glared at her.

After a long silence that the pack had made, a stunning Keeshond stood up. "What's this *village dog* doing here? We don't need any pampered dogs here, we already had enough." She snarled, glaring at the oldest canine of the pack. Her snout raised while her nose was scrunched up in disgust. She was one of the nastier council members.

Singing Crow shot her a glare, "I will explain later, but right now we need to honor the death of our packmate." She growled, her fangs bared as she gazed at one of the most trusted dogs in the pack. She had a temper but she knew what she was doing.

The female after a few seconds turned to her mate, Scrawny Raven. "Can you bring our visitor to the den, I'm not sure this is the best time to see our pack." She growled, focusing her gaze on the Weimaraner. Her eyes were cold, clouded with grief.

A Doberman Pinscher padded over to where they stood and flicked her docked tail. "Come with me, *youngling*." She murmured, a soft smile spreading onto her face. The alpha reminded Bumble so much of her mother, too much.

Paws stumbled as they pounded against the hardwood floor. Creaks were heard while towering bookshelves made a maze for the young pup. "Ma!" She called out, her voice frantic. Bumble felt so small among these books, her tail stuck behind her shivering hind legs.

No answer came searching for her, only silence.

"Ma?" She called out again, shrinking down. Her floppy ears pressed up against her delicate skull. She glanced over to her side, grabbing one of her jars of jam. "I guess if she's not here... I can always eat my jam!" Bumble barked, attempting to see the positive side of it.

The jam she had made this time was with her father and it was watermelon flavored. She had a friend who loves watermelons so she wanted to try it out and see what all the hype about it was all about.

She unscrewed the lid that had a plaid green cloth on it, throwing both of them aside. It was a beautiful shade of red, not too light and not too dark.

Bumble stuck her tongue into the jar and was overcome with sweetness. Bursts of energy shooting through her. It tasted like what Dewy Oak explained how it would taste! Amazing, delicious, life-changing.

"What are you doing, youngling?" A soft voice purred, it was her mother. She was a beautiful long-haired Weimaraner with smokey gray fur and olive green eyes. She was similar to her daughter, Bumble, but not by much.

"Earth to Bumble?" Scrawny Raven barked, her voice soft, not wanting to drive attention to herself. She gave a small sigh as she saw the female shuffle her paws and shake her head softly. "We should be heading to my den," She murmured.

"Oh, okay." She mumbled, a small scoff escaping her, upset with herself dozing off. "By the way, what can I call you?" Bumble asked, her head tilting to the side. "I know its a dumb question but uhm I want to know the answer to it?" She sounded unsure.

Scrawny Raven nudged her in the *correct* way to her den. "My name is Scrawny Raven but you can call me Raven if it's easier for you."

The dens were all made out of fallen trees, logs, or bushes. Twigs poked out of the bushes, a danger to pups who wanted to play 'swords' with each other. Their little pup games could be a bit dangerous at times.

"Okay!" She mumbled, her gaze darting around. Glasses making high-pitched sounds as they attempted to hit each other, like bickering pups. "What den is yours?" Bumble asked, her head tilting to the other side this time.

Scrawny Raven rolled her dark colored eyes, "Well, you see," She stopped at the large tree that had an entrance in the trunk. Vines crawling down the tree, flowers blooming. Foreign seashells lining the trunk. "This is mine and Singing Crow's den." She barked, a smirk crawling onto her face.

Her maw parted in awe, "It's... beautiful," She murmured. Her gaze soon went down to the seashells, her brow furrowed. "Where did you get those?" The female questioned. "I have never seen anything like those before." Bumble commented, continuing to stare down at them, ignoring the chaos.

"Well, I wasn't always a pack dog, you see." She mumbled, seeming ashamed of her past. "But enough about that, I found them near a beach in the place where *cherry blossoms* grow." Scrawny Raven explained, entering the den. Vines gracefully falling onto her back.

"I've never seen a cherry blossom before," She gasped, following the alpha into their den. The den had moss littering the ground along with feathers. Skulls and bones were also littered around. "This place is beautiful." She complimented, her eyes darting around.

"Thank you," The female murmured, her eyes soft as she gazed at the traveller. She plopped her rump down onto the moss, a small thud following. Her tail was swaying back and forth as her cropped ears pressed against her head. She was currently wearing a flower crown that had daisies. "It really is," She murmured.

Bumble tilted her head, "If you don't mind me asking, why did you invite me here?"

Scrawny Raven shook her head softly, "Me and my mate wanted to show our pack that outsiders aren't all bad but now with this sudden death I don't know how we'll do it." She mum-

17

bled, a small cry escaping her. Her eyes were clouded as she let them focus on her boulder-sized paws.

"I... I'm sorry for the loss you've experienced today..." Bumble mumbled, unsure of what to say. She's experienced many deaths but ran from them, not looking back. "I don't really know how to comfort you... but uhm I'm here if you need to talk about it?"

"It's fine, Bumble." Scrawny Raven mumbled, her voice shaking. "I must go say my blessings to him, if you want you may watch." She had to act tough for her pack, show them that there was nothing to worry about.

The stormy gray canine nodded, the den making her pelt darker. She would watch the pack make their blessings for the small elder. If they allowed her, she would make a blessing for him. Bumble didn't know much about how they did things but she could sure try to do it their way and show respect!

"May the earth bring you to the sky to hunt with our ancestors." Scrawny Raven howled, her front paw lifted. "Your wounds will stay but turn to something beautiful, resemblance of your death." She added onto what she was saying.

The other alpha stepped forward, "Your death should not be something to be ashamed of. May you accept it and become happy in the afterlife." She barked, her voice loud and clear.

Creek's head was bowed, not being able to say anything. No rookie was able to share their thoughts or the pups. Only ones with proper names. His tail was between his hind legs. Eyes wide, terror swirling around.

A day has passed and the body has been buried. Dogs were still grieving but some have gone on with their duties. Some were wary, unsure of what really happened to the dog. The dams would tell their worried pups not to worry and share pup tales with them.

Bumble lowered herself to the ground, nearing the Keeshond who had spoken up the day before. "Want some jam?" She asked, bowing her head at the council member. "I brought mango, pear, and apple jam this time!" The female told the canine, lifting her paw up.

"No, thank you." She growled, whipping her head to the side. "I won't take anything from you because for all we could know, you're gonna try to poison us!" Her lips were curled back in a snarl while her glare sharpened, sharper than thorns.

Scrawny Raven shook her head, walking away from her duties. "We really need to have the meeting soon," She mumbled to herself. "Gray Wind, she isn't going to poison us," The female growled, firmly. Her tail docked tail flicked as she stared at the lower ranking dogs.

"Are you sure she isn't?" Gray Wind snapped back, her ears flattened against her head. Her fluffy fur raised as she glanced back at Scrawny Raven and then at Bumble. The female's tail was raised.

Scrawny Raven let a small sigh escape her, "I'm sure she's not trying to poison us,"

"She could be though!" Gray Wing stuck to her opinion, too stubborn to change it.

A broad-shouldered female stepped forward, "Gray Wind, Scrawny Raven, Bumble." She barked, her voice cold. "Come to my den, we have something we need to discuss."

They both nodded and Bumble jumped in front of Gray Wind taking the lead out of the two. Paws tapping the ground as they followed. Snorts from pups were heard in the distance.

Gray Wind flicked her tail, "Let me guess it's about this little *village dog* here," She growled. Her tail was raised, fur following the new trend her body had. The female's nose was scrunched up in disgust as Bumble looked over her shoulder at her.

"I'm not a village dog!" Bumble objected.

Scrawny Raven shook her head softly, entering her den. "It is because of Bumble, you won't like what I have to say Gray Wind but you need to hear it."

CHAPTER THREE

He trotted forward, his head raised. "Any patrols I'm needed on?" Creek asked, his head tilting to the side. He would be happy to go on a border patrol but he knew no dog in their right mind would let a rookie on a border patrol.

"Jagged Paw actually wanted to teach you some herbs today." Rippling River murmured, dipping his head. His tail was swaying back and forth while his fluffy fur was raised. Even though his posture was aggressive his facial expressions were the complete opposite.

Creek tilted his head to the other side, "What... why?" He couldn't help but let disappointment swirl around his voice. He didn't want to learn about nasty herbs, he wanted to be out protecting and feeding his packmates!

"He said that it's important for our young dogs to know herbs," He mumbled. The male lifted a paw up and put it on Creek's paw. "Listen, pup, I know it doesn't sound great, but we all had to learn herbs even if we weren't going to be shamans."

Creek stepped away, his eyes focused on his smaller than average paws. "Fine." He growled under his breath, not wanting the male to hear him. "I'm guessing that I have to be there right now, so where are they?" He questioned, forcing a smile to crawl up onto his face. His tail was limper than a rock though, spilling his real emotions out.

"In their den," The Newfounland Dog answered. He flicked his fluffy tail over to a large rock that had a hollow entrance to it.

He has been in the shaman's den before and it was weird to him, who would want their den in the ground. There were ants and fleas in the ground, well he wasn't so sure about the fleas being in the ground. Even if there weren't fleas in the den, there were still *ants* in there. Next to spiders, ants were the worst thing to happen to the world.

The male turned his head slowly over to where the den was and a sigh escaped him. Paws pounding against the dew filled grass as he neared the shaman's den. "Oh, wow. Such beauty!" Sarcasm swirled around his face as his face dropped to a frown. "My favorite place to be!"

An older canine walked out of their den, moss clinging to her floppy ears. Flowers blooming from the vines that she wore on her crippled leg. She also wore a necklace made out of sunflowers. "Now, Creek can't you be a little bit nicer to those who heal your packmates?"

"The rock doesn't heal our packmates though...?" Confusion edged his voice as he furrowed a brow.

She shook her head softly, "It does, whether you believe it or not." The female softly barked, her voice shaking with age. Her tail was swaying back and forth, careful not to slam into the raging wind.

"Really?" He asked, his head tilting to the side.

"Really," She repeated.

A male trotted out of the den, rolling his charming brown eyes. "Stop putting that foolish pup tale into his head." His voice was deeper than the female's and Creek's. Well more like everyone in the pack. "You know what that did to Polar, he's off chasing fantasies now."

"It's not a foolish pup tale!" The blue canine growled, her floppy ears pressing up against her delicate skull. Tail raised along with fur raised. "You may be a good shaman but you don't know what's true; blinded by ignorance."

Creek stepped back, a small nervous laugh escaping him. "Should I uh leave...?" He questioned, continuing to step back. "Right now, doesn't seem like the best time to learn about herbs," Creek mumbled. Sunlight fought to get to his dark ginger pelt when he stepped back into the clearing of the camp.

"No, Creek, you need to stay," Jagged Paw barked. His tail flicked to the side as he looked away from the older canine with a sigh. "We'll just have to leave Cleared Sky alone," He growled. His eyes were narrowed each time he glanced over to Cleared Sky.

"Yes," Cleared Sky murmured, "Be an idiot and ignore the one who is right." Her voice was firm when speaking to the younger canines. She shook her head softly, walking away, mumbling something inaudible.

Jagged Paw whipped around, focusing his gaze on the den. "I'll lead the way," He barked. His tail flicking back and forth as Creek followed. Paws pounding against the dirt as they entered the den. Shelves were carved out, herbs put into their places.

"Still the dusty old thing?" Creek mumbled, shaking his head. He already hated it here. There was dirt everywhere and there also were holes for ants to crawl into. The herb stash didn't look like dirt which was good. His head tilted to the side as his gaze darted around, hooking onto each herb.

The male turned his head around, eyes hooking onto Creek. "Hm?" He had fluffy black fur but not as fluffy as Rippling River's fur. No one would beat Rippling River in this odd competition, he would always make it so his fur was fluffier.

"Nothing," Creek barked. His tail swayed back and forth as he struggled to set his rump down somewhere. He didn't want what happened to him earlier in his years to happen again. Those days were horrific. "Anyways, uh, what herbs will you be teaching about today?" He tried his best to sound interested but the boredom still made its way in.

"I will be teaching you about deadly herbs that you need to stay away from," He explained. His eyes darted over to where a leaf had many black dots, it was well hidden too, Creek didn't notice it till the male pointed it out with his eyes.

He tilted his head to the other side, "What are those things?" Creek questioned, taking a step towards it before being smacked with the shaman's tail. His nose scrunched up as he looked the male up and down.

"We do not eat those things, Creek." He barked firmly, hiding them with his body. At that moment, Creek realized that he wasn't only black but he had tan markings on his chest. His twisted paw raised as his glowing amber eyes pierced into Creek.

A small whine rippled into his throat, "Well, you can't tell me that we don't eat something without explaining why," He barked, pushing Jagged Paw to the side. The male grabbed a pawful of poppy seeds and swallowed them.

"No!" Jagged Paw snarled, pinning Creek to the ground. His lips were curled back in a snarl. "Oh my dog, why can't any of you rookies listen to simple directions?" He growled, letting go of Creek now pacing back and forth.

"To be fair you only told me not to eat them," He pointed out. The male still held a grin on his face while his tail slammed down against the dirt. For some odd reason, Jagged Paw in panic brought him happiness, knowing he wasn't the only one to panic when things went downhill.

Jagged Paw shook his head, his eyes tightly closed. "You'll be fine," He mumbled. "You'll be fine," He repeated. The male turned his head to look at Creek. "If you die, it's not my fault." They hummed, turning his back on Creek to let his gaze drizzle over his herb collection.

A few moments went by in pure silence.

"We already learned about one deadly herb, haven't we Creek?" The male chuckled, looking at the nails of his front paw.

His eyes widened, "Uh.... what?" He tilted his head to the side, furrowing his brows. "What do you mean by that? You didn't tell me anything was deadly yet!" Panic reached his voice as realization sunk into his body. "You didn't!"

"Well, you see you didn't let me explain why you shouldn't eat it," He mumbled, his old grumpiness coming back into him. His tail swayed back and forth, fur running down it like a waterfall. "So, it kinda sucks to be you right now, pup." He barked, a small laugh escaping him. "You remind me of your mother sometimes."

He curled his lip in a snarl as the male mentioned his mother. "Don't say anything about my mother!" Creek snarled, backing up; belly twisting. "She doesn't deserve to be spoken of! She's a traitor! A traitor I tell you!" He howled, continuing to back up.

"She's not a traitor." He spoke calmly. "She's just like our old Polar, chasing fantasies they will never be able to find," Jagged Paw explained. "It gets the best of us."

"That's basically what a traitor is!" He growled, refusing to see Jagged Paws view on things.

Jagged Paw shook his head meeting the male's gaze. "We're getting off topic," He mumbled. Plopping his rump down, he took a deep breath in. "Poppy seeds are toxic to us, it is very rare for a dog to die from them, but it is possible. Since you ate a pawful of them, you'll probably be passed out for about two days, I want to say." He explained, moving his paws when he spoke.

"Nice to know," Creek yawned.

He rolled his eyes, scoffing. "Are you taking any of this seriously?" Jagged Paw questioned him. "This is extremely important, you might need it in the future!" He pointed out, an edge to his tone.

"I'm taking it seriously!" Creek snapped. "Just because it doesn't look like it doesn't mean I'm not taking it seriously!"

"Mhm," He mumbled. "Anyways, parsley, is an amazing herb, it helps with our vision." Jagged Paw explained, pointing to each herb he talked about. "Also, another good herb is rosemary, it keeps those pesky fleas away," He told Creek. "I know how much you hate those things."

"I do hate fleas," Creek murmured, taking this whole shaman and herb thing in mind. This really could be useful, especially when fleas decide that they want to target him.

"And mint does-"

His eyelids started to feel heavy and the world started to spin. Paws wobbled as he struggled to stay standing up. "Jagged-" He only got to say the first name of the shaman's name before falling to the ground with a thud.

His breathing was heavy as he glanced around. He saw a younger him, carrying a sunflower in his maw. He was heading towards the nursery. The exact nursery where his mother had nursed him. The sunflower looked like it had better days too but it was still stunning.

"Where-where am I?" He stuttered, glancing around. Creek did not like this at all. No one was answering him, he was invisible to everyone.

The younger Creek stuck his head into the nursery. "Look ma, I found this for you!" He giggled, watching as his mother neared him. Her eyes were distant yet full of love. Only if the younger Creek knew what was to come. Destruction. Hatred. Disbelief.

"It's beautiful," His mother would purr, voice full of delight.

He threw his head up to the sky. "Take me out of here!" Creek howled, desperation circling his voice. "Take me out of here!" He repeated.

CHAPTER FOUR

"Can we at least keep her busy like border patrols so we aren't keeping her here for free?" A female questioned, gazing at the jam-selling canine. Her tail was swaying back and forth, letting her gaze eventually wander around, waiting for an answer.

Everyone was too busy talking to each other to notice her question. Bumble did notice her question though, but she wasn't able to answer it, since it was about her.

Poisoned Rowan started humming, "This didn't come from me but apparently her jam is amazing, a few of our pack members already tried some." This was for sure going to catch their ears, then she would be able to ask the question again.

A growl emerged from Gray Wind's throat as she whipped her head over. "Why would any of our pack members try her disgusting jam?" She questioned, her nose scrunching up while her ears were pressing up against her head.

Rippling River ducked his head, "Well, uhm, her apple jam is really good," He mumbled. "She adds cinnamon to it, I think!" He barked, tail swishing back and forth. His paws shuffled against the dirt of the council member den.

Gray Wind rolled her eyes, turning her gaze over to the large canine. "Really? Why would you even eat that disgusting jam?" She growled. "She could have been trying to poison us all." She exclaimed, jumping to her paws. Her ears were pressed up farther against her fragile skull.

"I would never try to poison anyone!" Bumble barked, shrinking down. Her paws were shuffling against the dirt. The female tail was wrapped around her, quivering at the accusation. "Why would I try to poison you guys? I have no reason to!"

"Sure, you have no reason!" Gray Wind snapped, now circling the female. Her tail was raised as her cold glare was exploring Bumble.

She tilted her head to the side. "Yeah, I know I have no reason!" The female purred, tail swishing back and forth. "Finally! I've been trying to tell you this all day!" A sigh soon escaped her as she jumped to her paws. Her floppy ears were perked up as a smile crawled up onto her face. "Thank you for believing me!"

Poisoned Rowan opened her maw to say something in response, but Drowning Shrew covered her snout with his tail, chuckling.

"Oh my dog, Bumble I am like super happy that Gray Wind here started to believe that," His voice had a high pitch tone to it as he spoke. Tail swaying back and forth as his long haired ears flicked to the side. The male neared Bumble putting a paw under her snout.

Bumble flinched at the sudden contact with the male. She didn't move back though, only met the *jokester's* gaze. "That's... uhm... great to hear...?" She slowly moved her head away, not wanting him to notice. Her tail flicked to the side as she glanced around, trying to meet one of the council members cold eyes.

Poisoned Rowan rolled her eyes, her black pelt shadowed. "Brother, don't do this to the newbie!" She scolded, a cackle of laughter escaping her. A bright green snake was wrapping around her neck as she was gazing at the female, it wasn't tight enough to hurt her though.

She had just noticed the snake, even though it was in plain sight. "Is that snake... harmful?" Bumble questioned. Her paw was raised as her nose wrinkled. Her tail wasn't swaying back and forth rather twitching as she watched the snake.

"He can be." The saluki cackled, winking. She brought her paw up, sliding her nail gently against the snake's scales. "Can't you, bean?" She purred, sharing a glance with her brother. Poisoned Rowan's tail was swaying back and forth as a smirk danced onto her face.

"What do you mean can be...?" Bumble mumbled, stepping back. She did not like these dogs. Why did she accept the alphas invitation? Was she sent here just to get killed by that horrific snake.

Rippling River rolled his eyes with a small sigh. "Ignore them," He murmured. "She's only joking around." He sent a growl towards Poisoned Rowan before glancing sweetly back at the tall canine. "Do you possibly want to go on a walk?" The male tilted his head, a small smile splattered onto his face.

Bumble glanced around at these *odd* pack dogs and gulped her saliva down, paws twisting out of anxiety. "Uhm, uh..." Her voice trailed off. "Sure?"

"That's great, so meet me at the camp entrance?" He asked, his tongue falling out of his mouth and resting on his shiny fangs. His tail was swishing back and forth uncontrollably. Rippling River snapped his head around, mouthing some words at his friends and sending a glare at them.

She nodded slowly before crawling out of the den. *I guess this is happening,* she thought, *He's not like the other council members though, not as weird as them at least.* Her paws pounded against the soil as she glanced around, wind dancing around her. Pebbles were scattered around, pressing against her paw pads when she stepped on them.

The entrance was a beautiful gorse tunnel, flowers blooming from it. At night, stars would love to tangle themselves into it, making it look like a fantasy world. Flowers were next to it too, pressing themselves up against it, wanting to be included.

"I do regret coming here but it really is stunning, I guess I could give it a chance." Bumble mumbled, glancing around in awe. Her tail was swaying back and forth as she continued to glance around. Paws shuffling against the soil when she waited for the large canine to come.

Thuds appeared, louder and louder as they came closer. "Hey! I'm so glad you waited for me!" He barked, a toothy grin spread out on his face. Floppy ears perked up and slobber running out of his mouth. "I'm sorry I made you wait this long though, I had to talk to the others for a few seconds." He explained, raising one of his large paws.

"And a few seconds turned into a few minutes?" She teased, noticing the male's soft gaze as he let it drizzle over her. His pelt color was different then hers too which made her more interested, he was brown and she was well a blue-gray color.

He shook his head softly, a small giggle escaping him. "Yeah, I guess, you're correct," He murmured. Wind was slamming against his large tail as it swished around, trying to control the wind. His tongue was in between his front teeth and it was a bright bubblegum pink with darker splotches.

Her eyes appeared smaller as a smile was ear to ear, she loved seeing other dogs happy.

"Ladies, first." He barked, voice delicate as he bowed down. Rippling River would be the kind of dog to put down his jacket for someone to cross mud, but he didn't have a jacket so whenever there's mud in the way, his body would do.

The glass made high-pitched squeaks as she skipped, looking over her shoulder at the monstrous sized canine. "We can have a picnic, if you'd like?" She offered, swaying her thin-furred tail back and forth. The female could go searching for berries and some meat, they could spread some of her jam on the meat, it's always good! Well, jam on meat was always good to her, she wasn't so sure about others though.

"That sounds lovely!" He barked, bowed down to his paws then quickly fixed his posture, not wanting to seem like a pup in front of her. His tail swishing back and forth even faster this time around. "What would we have at a picnic? I've never been to one." He tilted his head to the side, confused.

A gasp escaped Bumble as her head turned around abruptly. "You've never been to a picnic? Oh my dog, this is bad." She barked, taking a step back. "Like, really bad."

His eyes widened and his head was thrown around. "What's bad!? I can chase it away for you!" He barked, his dark colored gaze darting around. His stance was turned into a fighting stance as he jumped in front of the female.

"Oh!" She barked, jumping back in surprise. "I didn't mean it in that way, don't worry about what I said," Bumble murmured. Her tail was swaying back and forth as she gazed at him when he slowly turned around, confusion written onto his face. "So, uhm picnics are when you like hmm..." Her voice trailed off, trying to find a way to explain picnics.

A few moments passed and she opened her maw only to close it. She did this once again but she actually kept it open this time. "Well, picnics are when you talk with the other dog and share food!" She explained, cautiously. "We'll need some meat and berries, though." Bumble murmured, glancing around.

"I have some duck that I already caught earlier today." He chuckled, gazing up at the redwood trees that surrounded their every turn. "I can go that if you want?"

Her eyes widened and she shook her head. "Yeah, you can go get those, I already have berries I forgot about." She pointed out, watching him run in the opposite direction. "They were for jam but I can always get more," Bumble mumbled. She twisted her neck to make it so she could grab the jar of berries she had on her. It had all kinds of berries, strawberries, blueberries, blackberries, raspberries, anything a dog could name! Well, for the most part at least.

She set the jar down in the grass, it was clear and filled to the rim. This jar had a plaid pastel yellow cloth on it, all of her jars had different colors but they were all plaid and pastel. She absolutely loved pastels and how soft they looked.

"This is a good area, so we could probably do it right here." She told herself, plopping her rump down but she quickly jumped to her paws. She tilted her head to the side, not knowing if she should go grab leaves for the food or not. Bumble plopped her rump down again, deciding against it.

They weren't near the camp so no one should bother them, unless they were searching for prey or taking a small walk and accidentally stumbling upon the two.

A loud thud of paws came again. It was Rippling River. Anyone would be able to guess that though, he had the loudest paws, no one in the pack would be able to beat his record with it. Two ducks lay limp in his maw as he ran near her, skidding to a stop.

"Nice, ducks you got there." She barked, noticing how he was struggling to hold them with his teeth. Bumble had to hold herself from bursting out in laughter as he started to wobble over, glancing at the dead ducks like they were horrifying.

He shook his head, throwing them carelessly onto the ground, near Bumble. After he did that he coughed up many feathers.

"Let me help you pluck those feathers off those ducks," She giggled. Lifting a paw to snatch one of the ducks and pull it closer to her. Her tail was swaying back and forth as she started plucking the duck.

After, a while of both of them plucking the duck of all their feathers. She grabbed her jar of berries and opened it. "Want some?" She questioned, her head tilting to the side. Her tail was swishing back and forth much faster this time. "They're really good," Bumble added.

He poked his nail into the jar and ended up with a strawberry. His head now tilted to the side, the opposite of what Bumble's head had turned too. "What is this one? I've never had one of these." He barked, confusion filling his voice.

"It's called a strawberry, goofy." She barked, rolling her eyes. "Anyways, I have another thing we can try!" The female squeaked, jumping to her paws.

He shoved it in his mouth, gulping it down. "Oh okay!" The male barked, tail swishing back and forth. "Also, that *starberry* was really good!" Rippling River pointed out, raising his paw as he watched the female.

"Have you ever tried jam with meat?" She questioned, a smirk growing on her face.

"Jam with duck was very good," Rippling River barked,

soon letting a burp escape him. He dipped his head to apologize for his manners. "Anyways, what was the question you had?" He tilted his head to the side, gazing at the female.

Bumble opened her maw to speak but nothing came out. She tried again and something did come out, but not what the male had expected. "Who was the dog that uhm died…?"

Rippling River glanced away for a few moments before turning back to Bumble. "Well, uhm that rat was Short Aspen, not a lot of dogs liked him, but he was family nothing less." He barked, dipping his head in respect towards the dead canine. "Whatever happened to him, happened for a reason though."

A howl broke out and both dogs became alert.

Rippling River shared a glance with Bumble, a look no one wanted to see. The look of panic. "This is bad, we haven't had one of these howls in a while!"

CHAPTER FIVE

There stood a small Corgi standing over her limp pup. Tears streamed down her eyes and onto her squishy cheeks. Her long tail was stuck between her quivering legs while her rounded ears were pressed against her fragile skull. Sobs choking for every second that went by.

"What happened?" Bumble barked, her eyes wide with terror.

The female whipped her head around, "What did you think happened!?" Her lips were curled back in a snarl, showing sparkling fangs. "My baby is dead!" She growled, eyes filled with hatred and grief. The female's heart was racing, pounding against her chest.

Creek stepped back, his legs wobbling. This couldn't be an accident. First Short Aspen and now Chase. Whoever was doing this was a monster. Dogs will figure out sooner or later but they might not, it might have to be up to him to explore this mystery.

His legs gave up and he fell against a warm body. He twisted his head around to see a large male and he shrunk down. "Uh, sorry!" He quickly mumbled, jumping to his paws, hopping a spot away. His ears were pressed up against his head.

"It's fine," The male murmured, focusing his gaze on the mother and her pup. His tail was limp as he stared at them, tears hidden deep inside his body. This male never showed his emotions around others, it was like he didn't have emotions at all.

Creek nodded and plopped his rump down, silently.

Howls danced around the sky, in memory of the pup that passed. He would've been a great guard to the pack or even a hunter but he left them too early on. May he be a great pack member in the stars, dancing among their ancestors.

One of the alphas bowed her head to the mother, tears fighting back. The mother of the pup slowly backed up, gulping for air as she watched her pup be taken away from her.

The other alpha that approached left blue paw prints in the ground. She lifted her front paw and pressed it gently on the pups side that her mate was holding. "May you dance in the stars with your ancestors and may your scars turn beautiful," She murmured.

Howls began to dance once again, but louder and more stunning this time. They performed this ceremony everytime one of their kind died. It was important to them. This was how they sent their loved ones off into the afterlife.

Singing Crow flicked her tail to stop the noise. "Cinnamon, Jagged Paw, and Cleared Sky will bring the body and bury it at our beloved graveyard." She barked, laying the body carefully onto the soil, not wanting to harm it somehow.

Scrawny Raven stepped up beside her, raising her snout. "Also, just because we lost one of our packmates doesn't mean that we can slack on our duties." She barked, an edge to her voice now. "Kit, I want you to lead a border patrol with Red Fang and Hollow," She ordered.

The patrol grouped up, debating what border they would need to go on.

"Loud Tail, I know you're a guard but I know you have excellent hunting skills so I want you to take Timid Fawn and Creek on a hunting Patrol." She ordered, glancing around at everyone else. "Also, Rushing Cascade you can take Willow for a training session."

She turned back to the guards after a few seconds of hesitation. "Red Fang and Muddy Ears can guard the camp, then when they're done I want Drizzled Olives and Poisoned Rowan to take over." Scrawny Raven barked, glancing around. "Whoever is free please guard the nursery, we need extra protection there after what has happened today."

34

Creek was already sitting near Loud Tail so he didn't have to move and well Timid Fawn was all the way across the camp. She was a lanky Greyhound, but really anyone would be able to tell just by hearing her name. "I guess this was easy." He barked, noticing the female walk towards them.

"It really was," Loud Tail replied, not bothering to look down at the rookie. He was focused on the Greyhound who was walking over to them, since she was very flimsy, never able to take on much weight, ever since she was a pup.

The brindle and white female's tail was swaying back and forth as she struggled to keep her gaze focused on them. "I can't wait for hunting, what about you guys?" She questioned, tilting her head to the side, looking ready to hop off like a newborn fawn.

"I can't wait for it either!" Creek barked, attempting to share the same excitement she had. He ended up failing, but she didn't seem to catch on to it. Her paws were bouncing to each side as she stared at the two of them. His tail was swaying back and forth while a chuckle rippled through his throat.

A smile crept onto her face, ear-to-ear. "That's great! I'm glad I'm not the only one!" She barked, spinning in a circle now. Her tail was now a flash, faster than a lightning. Her paws were silent each time they slammed against the ground, it was a special skill she had mastered.

The Sarabi beside them rolled his eyes. "We should get going before we have a swarm of angry dogs swarming around us like a pack of bees." He advised, standing up. He shook his fur, little strands of fur flew up into the air, but not much at all.

"Yeah, I guess," The rookie mumbled. He wasn't too excited about hunting since he still wanted to try out border patrols. But no dog would even let him try, he'd just mess it up. His ears were perked as he watched the female bounce over to where the entrance was.

Timid Fawn rolled her eyes, long legs wobbling as she tempted to stay still. "Come on guys!" She barked, now bouncing up and down. "Gosh, males are slow pokes!" The female teased, sticking out of her bright tongue at them.

"We are not slow pokes!" The large male barked, looking offended. He had a playful tone carved into his voice as he chased after the female. Now, his paws were the opposite from the greyhound's, they were noisy and shook the whole earth, well Rippling River's pawsteps are much worse.

Creek rolled his eyes, "I'm a slow poke sometimes, so she's kinda correct." He chuckled, raising one of his paws as he spoke. The male quickly dropped it to the ground, following the dogs out of the camp. Paws slamming against the ground, dirt attempting to edge the tips of his nails.

She let out a small squeak, "I can agree with Creek!" Timid Fawn barked, a wink following. A bounce was in each step while her ears were perked up. She turned over to the large canine with a warm smile being painted onto her face. "What area are we going to, captain?" The multi-colored female questioned, her narrow head tilting to the side.

"Don't call me captain again, please, my name is Loud Tail." He stated, his voice flat. His tail was flicking to the side as he watched the trees cautiously. Paws avoiding the twigs that were scattered among the forest floor. Leaves threatening to crunch under his large paws. "We are going to hunt wherever the prey wants us to hunt," He barked calmly.

Timid Fawn opened her maw to object, but stayed quiet. Her legs wobbled as she stalked forwards, ready to strike if something ran by. She wasn't the best at balancing her weight onto the ground, always better at bouncing around, paws not always staying on the ground.

Creek tilted his head to the side. "Wouldn't it be better if we just chose one area to hunt in?" He questioned, stepping forward. A leaf crunched under his paw, leaving Timid Fawn to curse under her breath. Her tail was still swaying back and forth though, happiness always running through her bones.

"That wasn't the way I was taught to do it. I was taught to catch whatever was available." The male growled, keeping his voice low. Nose glued to the ground like a Bloodhound when tracking. Tail flicking to side-to-side when he tried to get a hold of a scent.

He bounced over to where the male was so he was right beside him. "Well, you are a guard so that might be why...?" Creek mumbled, shrinking down as the male's cold gaze swept over him, hurting more than frostbite.

"Just because I may be a guard, doesn't mean I don't know what I'm doing." He stated, whipping his head around to face what was in front of him. The male drizzled his gaze over on Timid Fawn, noticing she was shivering at the small argument he dipped his head in apology.

Creek shook his head roughly, his gaze sharpening. "I never said you didn't know what you were doing!" He barked, fury raging out of it. His tail was slowly raised, fur flowing down like a rushing waterfall on a stormy day.

"I know you didn't, but you basically said it in your own words." The male snapped back, continuing to walk forward, without a single paw stepping on a leaf or a twig. His tail was flicking side to side as his pace fastened. Nose twitching as a scent ran by him, a faint one though.

Creek rolled his eyes, he would just let defeat take over at this point. "Whatever, you say." He mumbled, taking in the passing scents of dogs that had crossed their paths. His tail was swaying back and forth, purposely swishing up leaves, to annoy the male.

"I will tear your tail from your body if you don't stop!" He threatened, a snarl edged in his voice. "We're supposed to be hunting, not scaring away prey." The male warned, bowing his head to passing leaves that got taken from the wind.

A whine crawled out of the graceful Greyhound as she continued to stalk forward. Her tail was tucked in between her shivering legs. "Can you guys stop arguing?" She whimpered, "We can't be splitting up in times like this." The female whispered, pointing out the recent deaths. Her ears were pinned against her head while her paws gently pressed themselves against the earth.

Creek dipped his head and let out a soft noise, it was a mix between a bird chirp and a bark. "Yeah, sure." He mumbled, lowering his belly to the ground. "Sorry," The male quickly added. Sunlight fighting through the trees and dancing on each of their backs, Creek's back now glowed because of it.

The leader of the patrol bowed his head, mumbling a small sorry.

She ignored the two and ran off, currently on a scent trail. The female turned her head around only to whisper to them. "Deer,"

The largest male out of the group jumped up, ears perked. Tail swayed back and forth, but other than that it was as straight as a branch could be. His paws were not making as much sound as they did as he fastened his pace. If they were able to take at least one deer down, he would be praised, since he was the chosen leader of this hunting patrol afterall.

Creek leaned forward, fastening his steps like the others. *This could feed the whole pack!* He thought ran around his head and he passed the monstrous male, the scent of deer teasing his freckled nose. Leaves swirling around him and the others, revealing the lonely female deer in the forest, grazing on some grass.

The male shared glances with the others in his patrol, giving them directions with his head and tail. They had to get this deer down. It would fill everyone for at least two days. He was gonna be the first to charge at the deer, then Timid Fawn, and of course Creek last.

Timid Fawn watched Loud Tail leap forward, startling the deer. He managed to use the deers moment of shock against her, biting onto one of its legs. The male didn't have the best techniques when it came to hunting deer, but if it got the deer down, whatever he did worked.

She shook her head, unable to watch it any longer and ran forward. Speed shooting through her as she nipped at the deer's sides. Her bites were effective, but not enough to harm the deer a lot. One of them would have to go for the throat.

Creek jumped over to the scene like a rabbit. The greyhound glanced at him, shaking her head towards the throat of the deer. He could be the hero in this! He could actually do something memorable if he didn't screw it up!

He stood there for a moment but then started to circle the deer. Lips curling back in a snarl, fangs sparkling as the sunlight hit him, but it was splattered sunlight due to the trees. He lunged forward, grabbing onto the deer's throat. Paws dangling as he dug them in deeper. Warm metallic tasting liquid crept into his mouth, wanting to make him gag, but he couldn't let go.

"You can do it!" The brindle Greyhound called out, repeating the process she was doing. She noticed the deer was getting weaker, so she made her bites sharper and more harmful.

In the back Loud Tail still held onto the deer's leg but had many painful wounds in his chest. He would end up going to the shamans' den when this was all over.

His teeth dug deeper into the throat, till the deer started to feel heavy and wobbly. He let go with a yelp as the deer started to fall. Blood splattered his snout, making him look like he just killed someone, well technically he did.

"Good job, guys." The male panted, wincing in pain. He had an open wound on her shoulder from being kicked multiple times. An almost inaudible sigh escaped him. "Now we have to drag it all the way back to camp..." His voice trailed off, disappointment drizzling it.

"Yeah, we did do a good job." Timid Fawn barked, pants escaping her. Tongue sliding against her fangs as she glanced down at the limp deer. Tail swaying back and forth, a smile emerged on her bright face. "It will be worth it though, our packmates will be really happy with what we brought back!"

Creek nodded at what they were saying. "Yeah, what Timid Fawn said," He yawned. Tail flicking side to side. The male bent his head down and hooked his teeth into one of the deer's crooked legs. His ears were pressed up against his skull as he started to attempt to drag it towards the place that they needed to bring it too.

Timid Fawn ran over to where Creek was pulling it and hooked her teeth in, helping him out.

CHAPTER SIX

Bumble watched wide-eyed as a group of dogs entered the camp dragging a plump deer. Her tail swished back and forth at the thought of everyone enjoying their meals. Maybe she could offer them jam to go with it! She had just made more jam not too long ago! So, now she had apple jam, pear jam, mango jam, and raspberry blackberry jam mixed!

One of the alphas, Scrawny Raven, stepped forward. A grin emerged on her face as she gazed down at the deer carcass. "The elders, the pups, and the dams will eat first like always but after, Loud Tail, Timid Fawn, and Creek will take their share." She stated, raising her snout and fixing her posture.

Her mate stood by her side, raising a paw. "May we cheer for the ones who brought us a great feast!" She howled, her voice stunning. Singing Crow's tail was swaying back and forth as she brought her snout down to gaze at the deer the three had caught.

"Loud Tail! Timid Fawn! Creek!" The crowd cheered, their voices wild and chaotic. Yelps were heard from the two pups who scampered over to the deer to sniff the unfamiliar prey.

Tails were swishing back and forth, slamming against the wind that tried to fight them. Excited barks continued to be thrown into the air. Paws thudding as they hit the soft earth, roughly.

The elders crawled out of their den, delicate bones creaking as they neared the prey pile. Paws being dragged or lifted, depending on the canine they were. Some still had their pride as an elder and some did not.

One of them instead of ripping into the deer, grabbed the rabbit that lay beside it. They wanted the younger canines to have the deer, after all they had more to live for. They had already lived their lives to their fullest now its the other pack members to live their lives to the fullest.

The pups tumbled over each other, wide-eyed at the sight of the big deer. "Ma!" One of them called, trying to tug a leg off. "Come help me!" He whined, his voice going high-pitched.

Bumble let out a chuckle, but quickly went silent when she saw Loud Tail's severe wounds. She trotted over to where he sat, admiring the dogs who licked their chops. Her tail was still as a rock as she neared while her floppy ears were perked up. "You should see the shamans."

The male looked as if he was going to argue but then he looked down at the wounds, wincing at the thoughts of them getting worse. "Yeah, I should." He mumbled, turning his back on Bumble. "But, I ain't gonna be doing it because you told me too," The male growled.

"Well, I don't care if it isn't because I told you too, at least you're getting the help you need!" She barked, turning her gaze over to the pups who fought over the leg the older dogs managed to rip off for them. Her tail was swaying back and forth and a smile grew like a budding rose on her face.

He rolled his eyes before heading towards the shaman's den in search for help. His tail was swaying back and forth behind him as he stole glances with a male.

She would probably be one of the last to get offered to join the feast, but she didn't mind. The female had already eaten something earlier so she wasn't as hungry as some of the others.

Creek was over in a corner with a small chunk of meat, deer, and a couple of mice he took from the prey mile. The other canine who took part in the patrol was off telling the story to a rookie, who eagerly listened. They both had some parts of the deer with them.

Everyone was going to eat well tonight and maybe tomorrow too! They wouldn't have to worry if they couldn't find as much prey tomorrow since they had a whole deer to feast on. Pups would probably sneak out in the night, chowing down on the deer as a midnight snack.

The alphas were sitting together, playing with the seashells that surrounded their den, unbothered to try to grab some prey. They made sure the pack was fed first, they wouldn't want to take something that their pack would need more.

Bumble stepped forward, cautiously sniffing the ground below her. She wanted some deer but she wasn't sure if she was allowed. Of course, if she couldn't have any deer she wouldn't mind. But, it would be nice if she could have some.

The female glanced over to where Poisoned Rowan sat with her brother and tilted her head. "Uhm, Poisoned Rowan...?" She called out, her voice shaking, noticing she still had the snake. Her tail went silent, not ushering a single movement.

"Hm?" She mumbled, in between bites of her meal.

She looked away, avoiding eye contact with the bright green snake. "Am I allowed to get some deer?" The female questioned, bowing her head, showing submission. Her tail was tucked and she lowered herself to the ground, expecting her to send her snake at her.

"Of course," She purred, stabbing the chunk of meat with her claw.

Bumble nodded and slowly backed up. She grabbed a hold of a chunk of deer and snatched it. She may as well run over to Creek, the first dog she had met in the pack. Her paws slammed against the grass as she skidded to a stop. "May I sit here with you?" She asked, her voice muffled from the meat that rested in her mouth.

"Yeah, sure." He mumbled, gulping down a mouse. The male gingerly tilted his head to the side as the female started to spread jam on her meat, it looked as if it was normal and completely okay to her. "Uhm, what are you doing?" Creek questioned, eyeing her up and down.

"Putting jam on my deer!" She barked, tail swaying back

43

and forth. Her ears were perked up as she continued to do it. "It's really good." Bumble told the male, stuffing some meat in her mouth. A jar of apple jam was sitting next to her, out of the vest she had always carried around.

"Oh, okay." He mumbled, his voice flat with no emotion layering it. "I don't really believe you when you say it's good but uhm, go off I guess?" His voice held confusion as he continued to watch Bumble. Ears flopping to the side while his nose twitched.

The female tilted her head to the side, confused on why he was disgusted. Jam on meat was amazing, it added extra sweetness the meat couldn't have on its own. "Why don't you believe me?" She questioned, her ears pressing against her fragile skull.

"I.. uh... it just doesn't sound that good..." His voice trailed off as he stared at his paws, unable to look the female in the eye. Creek's tail was curled over his paws as he ripped into another one of the mice.

She rolled her eyes, tail swaying back and forth. "You clearly don't have a good taste in food." Bumble snorted, continuing to munch down on the chunk of prey between talking. The female bent over and put her jam container in the slot it had, wary of Creek who did not like her wonderful meal.

"I do have a good taste in food!" The male shot back. "I just have common sense not to put something on food that doesn't belong there!" He barked, raising his snout, eyes refusing to look at the female. His tail was whacking his paws as he bent down and gobbled up the rest of his meal.

A howl broke out into the air and all the dogs were alarmed, yet excited. They didn't expect that this would happen today. It was the day that one would move up the ranks in the pack, a higher rank.

"May you all join in the center," Scrawny Raven barked, her tail swaying back and forth. The female's snout was raised as she looked down at the dogs who started to crowd around her and the council members, along with her mate, Singing Crow.

Barks of excitement came from the dogs, some even

bowed. Tails swished back and forth, slamming against the wind that fought back. Ears were perked up and smiles crept onto everyone's faces.

"Today is the day where two of our rookies become full members of the pack with respected names." Singing Crow barked, nails digging into the tree beneath her.

Barks came out of the crowd, exploding into the air.

"Willow step forward," Scrawny Raven ordered, catching the eye of a retriever who stepped forward. Her paw steps delicate and a flower crown falling off her head. It was made out of crumbling flowers, but the pups probably made it so she wore it. The female was one of the most motherly dogs in the pack even if she was only a rookie, well now she was going to become a full member.

The female raised her head, ready for a paw to come down her chest.

"You are now Ancient Willow!" She announced, a smile grew on her face as she saw the female's excitement. "*Ancient Willow* is now a Guard, who should be respected now that she has her name." She barked, her eyes sharp as she let them shower over the dogs. "You may back away into the crowd now." The female ordered, bowing her head.

Ancient Willow backed up into the crowd, her creamy yellow pelt attracting the sun that watched the canines from above, proud of their success.

"Creek, may you step forward?" Singing Crow questioned, her eyes scanning the male. Her tail was swaying back and forth, but slower then the others, not as excited. Once he neared, she ran her paw down his chest, causing him to bleed. "You are now Racing Creek, always chasing after your *dreams*, may that be passed on in our generations." She spoke, growling at the word 'dreams'. Her snout raised. "*Racing Creek* is now a hunter, y'all must respect him." She barked, her voice growing restless. "You may back up into the crowd now."

Bumble watched the ceremony, tail swishing back and forth. She had never seen one of these before! This was her first time visiting a pack, afterall. Maybe she could go ask Ancient Willow and Creek... no Racing Creek on a picnic! Maybe Rippling River would like to join too.

CHAPTER SEVEN

"Congrats, Racing Creek!" Bumble barked, her head tilted to the side. A smile was painted onto her face while her ears flopped over. Jam bottles continue to make high pitched sounds when they hit each other, like bickering siblings.

He couldn't say anything so he flicked his tail to the right. Once a dog becomes a full member of the pack, they are unable to speak for a day and if they do speak to someone, there's a chance that the canine would be punished.

"Huh?" The female took a step back, her nose scrunched up. She lowered herself to the ground as she gazed at him with watering eyes. "Are you ignoring me?" She questioned, a small whine rippling in her throat.

Racing Creek stayed silent, bowing his head down. Ears flat against his delicate skull; tail tucked in between his legs.

"Fine, ignore me." She barked, turning around, in search for Rippling River. Her tail was flicking side to side while her ears were now pressed against her skull.

He shook his head and turned around. She wouldn't understand, she wasn't raised and born into a pack, she was just a visitor. Sooner or later she would leave like the rest of the visitors. Paws thudding against the ground as he padded out of the camp.

Shrubs brushing up against his legs as he glanced around. He might as well look for clues on what could have been the cause for the murders. It was a stupid and hopeless idea but he wanted to try to find out, if he didn't end up finding any clues he would just go to hunting for the pack.

They never said what happened to the pup but everyone

figured it was berry poisoning. Creek could look at the poisonous berry bush for any chunks of fur on the thorns, everyone was told to stay away from there, ever since they were pups.

It wasn't that far from the camp, but still pretty deep into the territory. The berries were round like a grape, they also had spikes on them, yet a bright red color, a little lighter than the color of blood. They were deadly. It wasn't just poisonous, it was deadly. Within minutes for a young pup, they would have trouble breathing and if not treated, suffocate.

His fur was tugging at each other, it was either the violent wind or the bushes that he met on the way to the berry bush. Ferns were the almost common plant that had attempted to crawl up his leg and tickle him, there were some leaves that fell from the tall redwood trees who danced on his back. The sun was creeping down and joining the leaves.

The retriever couldn't even talk to himself, it wasn't just talking to others, but everyone. He loved talking to himself at times when he was alone with only the birds singing their songs. There were also the noises of the squirrels who ran down the trees, stealing acorns from the earth.

He was now near the berry bush, the red berries glowing as he approached. *Perfect.* His paws made the smallest thud when they hit the ground. Porcupines liked hanging out over here and he didn't want to get a quill on his rump *again*.

A patch of soft creamy fur was hanging from the bush. *What?* He questioned, glancing around before nearing the area. The male had to be careful whoever the fur belonged to, could still be lurking around.

He brought his nose up to it, careful not to stab himself. It smelt like roses. What kind of dog smells like roses? Roses had a disgusting smell, well at least to Racing Creek. Tail swaying back and forth as he tilted his head to the side.

The male could bring it back to the pack, but they would probably scold him. It would be better to leave it and go off and hunt. Hunting would do the pack better, then stalking around looking for clues to a death that probably was an accident.

He raised his snout to the sky, trying to find the scents that were swirling around in the air. There were squirrels and some moles that lurked around. He could probably go after some voles, it was one of the pup's favorite prey.

Racing Creek shoved his snout to the ground, following the scent. Paws pounding against the ground, but not enough to make the earth beneath him didn't vibrate. He would be fine for now but if the vole heard him, he would have to run after it. Afterall, his name was *Racing* Creek.

His eyes were tightly closed, letting his nose guide him. He didn't need to see where he was going, he had all of his senses, how hard would hunting without sight be? Racing Creek would just need to feel with his paws, balance with his tail, hear with his ears, and... sniff with his nose! It would be so easy!

Bang! His nose was pressed up against a tree, yet he decided to keep his eyes closed. The male slowly side-stepped it, tail attempting to help him balance. His paws were wobbly as he continued to follow the scents of the vole. He wasn't sure if it was a meadow vole or a pine vole. He hoped it would be a meadow vole since those were easier to catch.

A squeak was exposed to the air and his eyes shot open. He would catch it! He had too! The pups needed some vole meat again. Also, if there was another vole he would love to eat it. Voles weren't his favorite but they were still pretty good.

He snapped his jaws at it, but it ran off. The male wiggled his haunches and he leaped forward, drool falling from his fangs. His tail was swaying back and forth while his paws slammed down against the soft earth, getting closer and closer to the prey. He would do this, the pups needed it. He would catch it.

The male managed to swipe a paw at it, flipping it over on its fluffy belly. Now he would just need to pin it and snap its neck. Racing Creek flung his maw over to where he had struggled to get back onto its paws. He bit down into it, snapping its neck instantly.

The male flung it into the air and caught it. He didn't trust the wild animals around here, so he wouldn't bury his catch instead bring it right to camp then go back out again and continue to hunt. Tail swishing back and forth, he started to pad in the direction towards camp.

His brown eyes were wide with excitement, a hop in each step. His first day as a hunter and he managed to actually hunt something. This was the best day of his life. Too bad his mother wouldn't be able to see it, she was too pampered in her new village life.

The male's floppy ears perked up and then went down, the process was repeated many times. Shrubs would brush up against his legs, but he wouldn't mind. All that mattered right now was that he managed to catch a piece of prey on his first day as a hunter.

The vole swung around as he held it tightly in his maw. Should he just drop it off in the prey pile or give it to the pups? It was a hard choice. Since, the pups would play with his tail if he brought it to them but if he brought it to the prey pile some other dog might grab it.

His paw pads were covered in soil that decided to stick onto them. Pebbles that were scattered around the ground were unable to get in between his toes which he was more than grateful for. His ears were bouncing up and down as he started to hop to the camp, since he was right at the entrance now.

The pups would love him if they knew he brought it back but he decided he was going to put it in the prey pile. It would be easier for him and he would be able to hunt more and bring back more to the pack. They might catch his eye but it was unlikely, they were usually tumbling around the camp in fights with each other

He entered the camp, glancing around. Bumble was near a den, talking to Rippling River and well the pups were nowhere to be seen.

A yelp escaped him, tiny teeth digging into his tail. That's where the pups are. He dropped the vole and let out a sigh. Looking behind him, a smirk crawled onto his face as he directed them to the vole with his paw.

The pups let go of his tail easily racing over to the prey. Tumbling over their own paws as they argued over it, trying to decide who was going to get it. A small grief stricken Corgi walked over to them, telling them off. The dam made things better when they weren't and here she was, filled with grief and tiredness.

Racing Creek dipped his head and quickly turned around. Tail swaying back and forth as he neared the exit of the beautiful camp. Paws pounding against the grass as he fastened his pace. He would probably go to the Owl Tree, where the owl sleeps is where the mice lurk around.

His ears were perked up, listening to the leaves crunch the paws of woodland creatures seeking for shelter away from their enemies. Racing Creek glanced around, his ginger pelt slowly warming up from the sun that danced around the sky, fighting off the clouds who threatened them.

He closed his eyes for a short second. "I know I'm not supposed to talk, but am I supposed to journey to the villages? What if my mother had something to do with this...?" The male mumbled to himself, the scent of a dog meeting his quivering nose.

Moose scraps! He thought, panic running through his body.

"I'm not going to let some *rookie* off on their own to a village." The voice barked with a small chuckle. "Now am I?" He questioned, gazing at Racing Creek with a smile creeping onto his face. His tail was swishing back and forth as he continued to look at Creek, waiting for a response.

"Ugh, fine, I guess." He mumbled, looking up at the sky. "We'll have to leave now though," Racing Creek barked. His tail was limper then a broken twig. "We can't take the chances of being caught."

CHAPTER EIGHT

"I feel bad now," Bumble mumbled. Her gaze was fixed on her paws as she leaned against the large male who sat beside her. His fur was hiding half of her body due to how fluffy he was. Her tail was limp, not swishing back and forth like it usually was. The vest she usually wore was resting in the alpha's den.

Rippling River nuzzled her with a small sigh falling from his mouth. "You didn't know that's what we did, I'm sure he doesn't mind that you got upset." He murmured, his voice soft when he spoke to the female. His tail was curling around her and his ears were pressed up against his skull. The male's skin was slowly warming up too.

Bumble shook her head, pulling away from him. Her eyes were restless as she dug her nails into the dirt. "It's not fine! I shouldn't have assumed things!" She barked, her voice going high-pitch and cracking when she spoke. Her eyes were starting to water up and she glanced over at the council member. "Sorry."

Rippling River set his head on her head, attempting to calm her down. "All is fine, he'll be here soon and you can apologize then." He murmured, focusing all his attention on the female. "He may not be able to accept it right away but I'm sure he will once he's able to talk." The male reassured her, his tail swaying back and forth.

"Okay," She mumbled, letting her eyes close as each second went by. Right now, she could end up passing out on the ground. Her tail had the slightest swish to it as she leaned farther into the male's fur. Her head was starting to feel heavy while her body was cradled by the wind, almost as gentle as a giant's touch.

A small giggle crawled out of Rippling River as he watched her start to fall asleep. "Don't fall asleep on me," He murmured. "I wouldn't want you to sleep somewhere that's not comfy." He barked softly, letting her lean into his thick fur.

Her eyes blinked open, vision blurry. A shiver ran down her spine as she stood up, her paws wobbly. Her maw parted in a long yawn, dagger sharp teeth shimmering. Nails digging into the soil beneath her when she arched her back, stretching her bones.

In front of her was a big brown blurry figure. The figure held something in his maw but she couldn't figure out what it was.

She blinked once more, her gaze returning to normal. Her ears perked up and her tail was swishing back and forth. The female's eyes were bright and a toothy smile met her lips. "Red!" She howled, running into Rippling River as she noticed that he was holding her plush.

"Oh, so this is what you called this strange thing?" He chuckled, dropping the plush at her paws. A grin was shown on his face as he watched her excitement towards the plush. His tail was swishing back and forth as he gazed into her stunning green eyes.

She tilted her head, confused at why he called the plush strange. "It's not strange, it's a plush!" Bumble barked, bending down to grab it with her sharp fangs. Her tail was swishing back and forth even faster this time. "It's a booby plush!" She was looking down fondly at the bird plush.

"Oh, okay!" He barked, slightly rolling his eyes. His thick fur was being pushed around by the air and he let out a sigh. His tail was still swaying back and forth though while the trees hid the sunlight from reaching his pelt and warming it up. "By the way, we're needed on a border patrol!" He barked, forcing a smile upon his lips. His ears were pressing up against his head, he hated border patrols with a passion.

Bumble nodded, holding onto her booby plush tightly. "So, uhm what's a uh border patrol?" She asked, stumbling on her words as she spoke. Her tail was still swaying back and forth as she stared at him with eager eyes. A smile was still on her face when she tilted her head to the side.

"A border patrol is when a group of dogs patrol and mark their territory." A voice broke in and she recognized it as Scrawny Raven's. Her docked tail was raised along with her cropped ears, staring at the two dogs who stood, talking. "I will be joining your border patrol and Rippling River will be leading it." She stated, her voice collected and calm.

Bumbled nodded, glancing over at Rippling River then back at the alpha. Her floppy ears perked as she kept glancing back and forth between ehr. Her teeth were clutching onto her plush even more, frightened that she might lose him again. "When will we be going?" She questioned, her head tilting to the other side now.

"Right now," Scrawny Raven barked, turning her snout over to the exit of the camp. Admiring its beauty as she stared at it. Her docked tail was still raised but her cropped ears rested, unable to stay confident like the rest of her.

Bumble bounced into the air with a small pup squeak. "Okay!" She barked, her voice continuing to be muffled since she still held the plush in her maw. Her tdail continued to swish back and forth as she watched the dogs among the camp share the latest gossip.

"Rippling River, what border will we be patrolling today?" The female asked, staring at the male with a cold look. She furrowed her brow as she waited for an answer to appear.

He opened his maw to say something but shut it quickly. His ears were slowly pressing up against his head as he watched the alpha's every movement. "We'll go to the border near the coyote's den." Rippling River barked, his voice low and almost inaudible.

"Shall we, then?" She chuckled, waiting for the canine to take the lead. The female rolled her eyes as the male stood where he was. "You're supposed to be the leader of this patrol." She growled, her tail twitching.

He nodded and jumped into the lead, averting his gaze down to his paws. His fluffy tail was swishing back and forth, strands of fur flying into the air. "Yeah, I know that, I was just uhm testing you." He covered up his naive brain with that silly excuse.

"We all know you didn't know, River." Bumble chuckled, watching his tail with fascination. Even though the alpha was being stern and testing his limits, he was still wagging his tail like nothing happened. A strange one indeed. Her paws made the smallest sound as they hit the ground.

Rippling River jumped up and grabbed a daisy that was blooming from the exit of the camp. He turned around and put it behind the female's ear with a small cheeky smile. "Just for you, m'lady." He murmured, running back to where he was supposed to be.

Her blue-gray fur glossy as she walked. She looked up at her ear, smiling at where the flower rested. Bumble's tail swayed back and forth and a yawn escaped her as they padded out of the camp. Silence danced along the backs of the canines. "So, uhm how do we mark the border?" She questioned, breaking the eerie silence between them.

"Well, uhm we'll show you when we get there." Rippling River murmured, tail swaying back and forth. He glanced over to where Scrawny Raven followed him. He mumbled something inaudible to the female and the alpha shook her head softly.

The female jumped to her paws, thin-furred tail swaying back and forth, faster than lightning ever dared to go. "Okay!" She barked, still clutching onto the plush that rested in her maw. It was rather soft for being thrown around in the forest. Bumble had got the plush at Shimmering Stars Village, they have plushies for good luck and she was gifted one.

Paws were thudding against the ground as they neared the border. Stale coyote scent reached all of their noses as they continued to walk.

Bumble continued to have a bounce in her paw as her gaze darted around. She had to be on the lookout for things she could use for her jam. She opened her maw quickly. "Is there any jam you suggest I make?" The female questioned, bringing her gaze up to the daisy that was still resting behind her ear.

"We have a chestnut tree not too far from here," Scrawny Raven pointed out. "You can always make jam made out of chestnuts." She barked, a smile meeting her face. Her docked tail was swaying back and forth as she kept her gaze on the young canine, warmth was swarming around in them. The female's paws were the second to lightest out of the patrol, only slamming down when she wanted to scare a crow from coming near.

Rippling River nodded, his tongue lolling out of his mouth. "That's a good idea!" He barked, tail swishing back and forth even faster. The wind had been slicing through his thick fur, sending a cool exposure to him, relieving him from the warmth that was hidden under all of his pelt.

"I think I'll do it soon!" She murmured, excitement glowing from her. Her eyes were glancing around, trying to catch sight of the abandoned coyote den.

Scrawny Raven let out a small giggle. "We're almost there." She barked, noticing that the female was growing curious about her surroundings and where everything was placed. Her ebony colored nose was quivering as a small droplet rested on it, too careless to move for the alpha's comfort.

"Oh okay!" She barked, hopping over to walk beside the alpha. Her tongue was close to sliding in between her teeth but she stopped it. She didn't want to seem like a fool in front of everyone, now did she? Bumble's ears did pin back though as the stale scent grew stronger, it was still stale but stronger. "I hope you don't mind me asking, but who is Birch?"

"Birch... hmm thats a hard one to say but uhm he's actually my son." She murmured, closing her eyes as she spoke. Her tail was swaying back and forth. "He's also next in line to become alpha." She barked, her voice almost silent as she spoke.

Any dog could see the fear running through her eyes like a rabbit running from a fox, terrified. A small whine rippled from her throat. "But, there's a twist to this whole thing..."

Rippling River bowed his head, plopping his rump down as the alpha spoke. His tail stopped swaying back and forth and curved around his body.

"He's blind," She mumbled. The female stared at Bumble, her eyes dark. "With him being blind leaves him vulnerable because many would challenge him for his position." The female barked, her tail flicking side to side. "I'd like you to meet him someday, you two would get along well."

Bumbled nodded but tilted her head to the side quickly after. She didn't get all these terms they used in packs but it seemed interesting. "Uh sure!" She barked, running in ahead of Rippling River. "I'd be happy to meet him!"

Scrawny Raven let out a small giggle at the female's excitement. "That's good to hear," She mumbled. The female glanced around, a sigh running out of her. "We're here!" The female announced, glancing over to Rippling River who was trying to stand up without accidentally falling down for the fifth time. The female bowed her head to Bumble who was shivering in excitement. "Rippling River and I will get it done real quick and then we can head back."

Bumble nodded, watching them rub against the trees, grass, and marking their territory. Her tail was swishing back and forth as she waited for them. While waiting she glanced up at the trees and for once in her life she thought about staying put in this pack but living in a tree like a squirrel. She'd probably end up changing her mind, since she was born to travel the world. The female was still holding onto her red-footed booby plush but her grip was loosened now.

Rippling River and Scrawny Raven padded over, their heads raised high. "We're done so we can head back." The newfoundland barked, his tail swishing back and forth as he gazed at the female and how she still had the flower behind her ear.

Scrawny Raven tilted her narrow head, furrowing a brow.

"Would you like to meet Birch when we get back to the camp?" She asked, focusing her gaze on the female. Her docked tail twitched as she waited for an answer from the young canine.

"I'd love to!" Bumble barked, bowing down, her eyes playful. Her eyes were wide while excitement danced around her beautiful green eyes. Eventually, she would get to meet the whole pack! Tail swaying back and forth as the thought raced around her mind.

The female dipped her head in response. "Well, we better be getting back to camp then." She barked, her voice soft as she spoke. Her docked tail swished back and forth as her paws hit the soft earth. A grin was fixed onto her face as she looked forward. Her posture was perfect as she walked, she probably had the best posture out of everyone in the pack.

"Yeah!" Bumble barked, her voice still muffled as she carried the plush with her. Her tail was swaying back and forth while her ears bounced up and down. The female's whole body was shaking as she hopped ahead of the dogs who were in the patrol.

Rippling River gave a simple nod.

"Birch, this is Bumble as you already know." Scrawny Raven murmured, setting her gaze on the heir to the pack. Her head was raised, showing dominance as the dogs surrounded around, poking their heads out of curiosity.

The male gave a simple nod, his long fur swaying back and forth as the wind danced around him. His beautiful brindle fur was attracting the sun to climb down from the treetops, not regretting their journey to get down there.

The alpha glanced over to where Bumble sat. "Bumble, this is Birch." Her voice was soft like she was talking to her pup. With others she brought off a cold demeanor but with Bumble it was different.

CHAPTER NINE

"Are you sure we're going the right way?" Loud Tail questioned, his brow furrowing as he gazed at the younger canine. His tail was swaying back and forth as his paws made the slightest pounding sound against the dew filled grass. Last night it had rained and soaked the grass, along with the dogs. His fur had dried quickly but Racing Creek's not so much.

Racing Creek nodded, continuing to shake his fur, attempting to get the wetness off of him. It felt like a bunch of creepy crawlies were prowling for prey in his fur. His tail was swaying back and forth as he walked, keeping pace with the male beside him. "We are!" He barked, offended by the male asking if he knew where they were going.

The truth is that Racing Creek had no clue if they were going the right way, to his knowledge they could be lost.

Loud Tail nodded, keeping his eye on the male. "Yeah, sure we are." He chuckled, shaking his fur. He eyed Racing Creek up and down with a roll of his eye. "You look like a rat that has been drowned-" The male barked. "-twice." He quickly added, a smug look emerging on his face. His tail was swaying back and forth as a giggle escaped him.

His lips curled back in a snarl and his eyes hardened.

The male wiggled his haunches and jumped into a mud puddle that was near Racing Creek. Water splashed, soaking Racing Creek even more than he already was. A smirk was painted on his face as he ran ahead, glancing behind his shoulder to see a furious retriever.

"You're going to pay for this!" He growled, jumping after the male while trying to shake his fur at the same time. Racing

Creek was a strange one, for sure. His tail was swaying back and forth as he chased after the male. His paws were making splashing sounds as they slammed into puddles, droplets flying onto his fur.

He turned around, a smirk still splattered on his face. "We'll see about that!" The male called out, glancing up at the redwood trees, some of them had branches lower to the ground. He jumped up as the male started to catch up to him and tugged on the branch.

Water came pouring down onto the two dogs. Racing Creek appeared more annoyed than before and Loud Tail was on his back laughing.

The Sarabi dog jumped to his paws, rolling his dark colored eyes. "Anyways, why are we going to this village? All I know is that it's something about your ma?" Confusion tinted his voice as he tilted his head to the side, staring at Racing Creek. His tail was swaying back and forth as his ears pressed back.

"Well, uhm, you know those two murders that happened...?" His voice trailed off as he spoke.

The male nodded in response.

"I think that my mother was involved in it," He stated. Racing Creek took a deep breath in and released it, ready to speak once again. His snout was raised high as he gazed into the eyes of the tall male. The male's tail was swaying back and forth. "I... uh... uhm... think that if we go to this village she's in... we'll be able to find some clues that can get us ahead in this mystery." He barked, trying to seem hopeful with his plan. The truth was, he wasn't very hopeful about his plan, but there was still a small spark of hope dancing within him.

Loud Tail slowly nodded, closing his eyes. "Okay, I don't think your mother had something to do with this, but I'll still travel to the village with you." He barked, dipping his head. The male looked up at the sky, stormy gray clouds covering the sun. "We should find shelter though, before night hits." He suggested, nose twitching at the scents that swirled around.

"Thank you, it means a lot." Racing Creek murmured, putting his snout under Loud Tail's. His tail was not swaying back and forth rather swishing back and forth, like the speed of lightning. This wasn't like the old days, where Loud Tail teased him as a pup, they were working together, like a team. "And, yeah we should go find shelter." He murmured, a smile painted onto his face.

Loud Tail pulled away, searching the area for a possible den site. "Do you think that badger den is still intact?" He questioned, furrowing a brow. His head was tilted to the side, continuing to let his gaze dart around the forest. They were both still in the redwood forest, but close to exiting.

"It should be, the rain wasn't that hard." Racing Creek replied, letting his eyes follow Loud Tail's. He attempted to shake the water off of him once again. The male lifted his paws one by one shaking the water off them. Water was one of things he hated, along with ants. *Did he really have to do this?*

Loud Tail nodded and set off in the direction of where the den would be placed, his tail swaying back and forth, glancing behind his shoulder to see if Racing Creek was following. His tongue lolled out of his mouth, drool splattering onto the grass.

"Hey, wait up!" Racing Creek called out, his paws threatening to slip on the mud. His eyes were bright as he chased after the male. His ears were perked up when he listened to the birds singing their songs. Squirrels were taking shelters in their homes in the trees, nibbling on the nuts they had found.

A small playful growl rippled in his throat. "Well, you better start running faster, slow poke!" He called out, his paws slamming down onto the ground, soaking up the water. His tongue continued to loll out of his motu, chunks of drool falling to the ground with a splat.

"I'm not a slow poke!" Racing Creek replied, making his pace go faster. His paws were barely touching the ground when he chased after the male. The male's tail was still swishing back and forth, faster than the speed of lightning. His handsome eyes still focused on the male ahead of him.

Loud Tail let out a chuckle. "Oh, yes you are!" He barked,

his ears flicking as his heart pounded against his chest. The male was slowing down, losing stamina very quickly. His paws were getting louder as each second went by, soon being dragged.

"Now, who's the slow poke?" Racing Creek taunted, furrowing his brow. A smirk was crawling onto his face as he slowed his pace, walking up to the male's side. His fur was swaying back and forth from the wind that was dancing around them. Shivers ran down his spine while the water on him refused to dry. Even though he was freezing, his tail swayed back and forth.

The male just rolled his eyes. "Well, for the record I'm way faster than you are." He replied, raising his snout stubbornly. His ears were perked as the den came into sight. It was dug into the trunk of a tree, it should fit Racing Creek but the Sarabi Dog was way too big for it. "Found it!" He howled, restraining from doing it loudly though, they could easily be caught by the pack.

"Oh!" He barked, running in a quick circle. His maw parted in a silent yawn as he followed the male to the den. A bounce was in each step of his, but he kept attempting to shake the water out of his fur, almost falling. The male leaped into the badger den, dirt mixing in with his wet pelt. He laid down, paws shrinking into his pelt.

"Have a nice night," The male whispered. He laid down, resting by the tree that the den was placed. His tail was curled over his back paws.

Racing Creek tilted his head to the side, a small mumble escaping him. "Why won't you climb in here with me?" He questioned, his voice muffled as he tried not to drift into a deep sleep. His tail was swaying back and forth as he tried to peek out of the den.

"I'm too big for the den," He told the male, sorrow filled his voice as he saw sadness dance around Racing Creek's eyes. A sigh escaped Loud Tail and he bent down, crawling into the den Racing Creek was laying in. Dirt was falling onto his back as he attempted to crawl in.

Racing Creek didn't even notice what was happening

since slumber had already taken over him.

He curled his whole body over Creek, protecting him while they slept. He closed his eyes, yet kept his ears perked, in case dangers neared them. The male refused to fall asleep but sooner or later he would drift into a light sleep.

"Wake up." Creek mumbled, poking the male's belly. His tail was swishing back and forth as he tried to get out from beneath the heavy canine. He grunted, unable to get out, the male was too heavy and he was on Racing Creek. "Wake up!" He groaned, attempting again to push the Sarabi Dog off of him.

The male's eyes flickered open and he pushed himself to the very side of the den. He tried telling Racing Creek that it was too small the night before, but did he listen? "I'm going, I'm going." Loud Tail mumbled, waiting for the dog to get out of the den so he could crawl out after him.

Racing Creek waited for the canine to crawl out, his tail swishing back and forth swiftly. He ran in a quick circle as he noticed that the male's head was poking out. The male bowed down, a playful growl running down his throat. The wetness on his pelt had dried during the night.

Loud Tail rolled his eyes, a small chuckle following him as he managed to get out of the den. It sure was a tight squeeze for him. He shook his pelt, dirt being thrown into the air, some hitting the Hunter. A growl came from his stomach, but he ignored it. "What's got you so excited?"

"Remember what happened last night?" He questioned, his head tilting to the side. A smirk was being painted onto his face. His tail was swishing back and forth, even faster this time.

Loud Tail nodded, backing up slowly till his body slammed against the tree. "Uhm, yeah..." His voice trailed off as he realized where this was going to go.

"Well, watch out, revenge is only one step away!" He barked, cheerfulness swirling around his voice. Racing Creek whipped around, a smirk still mixed onto his face. "We have to get going now, the village isn't too far away!" He barked, bouncing to where he thought the village was going to be.

"Where is the village that we're heading too?" He asked, tilting his head to the side. He didn't mind what village they were going to go too, but there might be a way he would be able to help if he knew what village they were heading too.

"Shimmering Stars Village," He barked. His tail stopped swaying back and forth as he spoke. His ears perked as he shoved his nose to the ground, following the scents of that led to warm cottages and baked pies. The male would end up breaking some rules though, since there would be some amazing food there that he might be able to try. Also, shopping! He could shop all he wanted too and have a bunch of accessories on him! Being there would be amazing.

Loud Tail shook his head roughly. "I believe that's near, there's also a mushroom forest close to that one I believe?" He sounded uncertain with his choice of words. The mushroom forest was home to the dogs who danced in the Pointed Mushroom Village. He had been in the mushroom forest once, but long ago when he was only a pup. The male held faint memories of that place.

"Yeah, there is a mushroom forest by that village, the elders used to tell me all about it." He murmured, lifting his snout only to put it back onto the ground. "I believe Cinnamon was from that village." The male commented; Redwood trees started to fade as they entered the new forest, a forest with oak trees and birch trees. Meadows were dancing around, making it clear that the dogs would be able to see the stars at night if they wanted too.

"I can see why they call it the Shimmering Stars Village now." Loud Tail commented, gazing ahead at their territory. His tail was swaying back and forth as he followed Racing Creek.

Voices neared, there was one both of them were able to make it out. "Ugh, what do these pack dogs want?" The voice was almost inaudible but loud enough for dogs to hear if they were nearby.

Both of them froze where they were standing.

CHAPTER TEN

"Have you guys seen, Racing Creek?" Bumble asked, her head tilted to the side as she stared at all the council members. Her tail was curled around her body and her gaze was soon moving down to her paws. She had an extra weight on her once again, since she was wearing the vest that she kept all the jam in and she managed to make another slot in it for her plush.

Poisoned Rowan shook her head softly. "I haven't seen Loud Tail either." She replied, worry spiking in her voice. Her head was dipped as she gazed at the Weimaraner; her tail was curled around her body, tighter than Bumble would be able to do.

"Aw, little Rowan can't see her crush." Poisoned Rowan's brother taunted, his voice soft as he circled the female. Tail swaying back and forth as his eyes darkened when he noticed her glow in the dark snake hissing at him. He rolled his eyes at the snake, ignoring its presence.

"I don't have a crush on him." She growled, glaring at her brother. Her tail was whipping back and forth as she whispered something to her snake, Bean. Her lips curled back in a snarl, teeth shimmering as the sunlight fought back into the den.

He rolled his eyes. "Yeah, sure you don't." Drowning Shrew mocked, giggles escaping him. Tail swaying back and forth as he dragged his claw along her chest. A smirk was dancing on his face as he plopped his rump down, staring at those who sat in the den.

Gray Wind shot a growl towards one of the twins. "This isn't the time for games, Drowning Shrew!" She snapped, her ears pinned back. "Two of our packmates could be missing and you're over here teasing your sister." She continued to growl at the snowy white male. The fur on her back was bristling as she glared at him. "They could be in serious danger!"

The male took a step back, his lips now curling back in a snarl. "Well, at least I know how to bring up the mood when something bad is happening, Miss, Pessimistic." He snarled, standing up, he was towering over the smaller female.

"I'm not a pessimistic, darling." She growled, facing the male. "I just think realistically and when something bad is happening I don't fool around, I try to get what happened, back to where it should be." Her voice grew sharper with every word she said, it soon came sharper than the blade of a dagger.

His twin sister stood up in defense of her packmate. "She's right, Drowning Shrew." She growled, now nose to nose with the male. "You're fooling around while our friends are missing, what kind of dog does that make you?" She didn't wait for him to answer, but continued on talking. "I don't get why Singing Crow and Scrawny Raven even gave you a high rank in this pack if you're going to act this way!"

Her brother rolled his eyes. "You're being a hypocrite." He growled, his gaze darkened and narrowed. "You're always goofing off but now when I'm goofing off, it's a problem?" The male shook his head, a small chuckle escaping him. "Well, I'm not goofing off actually, this is how I always act, I don't have fake personalities like you."

She flinched, but did not move her cold gaze away from the male. "If you're going to try to insult me, it's not going to work." The female stated, calmly. Her tail was raised, confidence dancing around her.

Rippling River nudged Bumble out of the den, hoping the others wouldn't notice him and Bumble sneaking out. His tail was swaying back and forth as he crawled out of the den, glancing around at the camp. "Do you still have that flower I gave you?" He asked the female, head tilting to the side.

Bumble nodded, grabbing the flower out of the slot that the plush was. It was crumbled but still intact. "Yeah, I still have it, why?" She questioned, her voice muffled. Her gaze was darkened as she gazed down at her paws, avoiding eye contact with the male who stood in front of her.

"Just wondering." He barked, resting his tail on the female's back. Rippling River bent down his head so he could be side to side with Bumble. "We can go look for them if you want," He suggested. His tail was gentle, softer than a feather.

"I would like that," She mumbled, still carrying onto the daisy that he had given her the day before. "Do you have any idea on where they would be?" Bumble asked, her head tilting to the side. The female's tail was swaying back and forth as she waited for Rippling River's response to her question.

The male shook his head softly. His chocolate brown fur was burning from the sun that slow danced on his back, hopping onto Bumble's back. "I don't know..." His voice trailed off as he spoke. He let his gaze lower to the ground. "Sorry."

"You don't have to be sorry for anything." Bumble barked, licking his cheek. Her tail was swaying back and forth as she fastened her pace. Paws not making a single sound as they hit the ground, avoiding all the puddles that were littered around.

His eyes widened, stumbling back in shock. "Wait!" He called out, running after the female. "Also, I do have to be sorry since I don't know where they could be." Rippling River mumbled, as they both neared the exit of the camp, their tails swaying back and forth.

There was a large puddle in the way of getting out. Rippling River rolled onto it, covering the whole puddle so Bumble could get out of the camp. His belly fur was soaking up the water, more and more because Bumble stood there, staring at him.

"Uhm... what am I supposed to do?" Bumble questioned, continuing to stare down at him with wide green eyes. Her tail was still swaying back and forth and her ears were perked up. "Also, why are you in the puddle? Aren't you cold?" She questioned, concern dancing around her voice.

"Well, uhm I was doing this so you wouldn't get your paws wet." He answered, his voice muffled. Rippling River continued to wait for the female to climb over him so he could get up.

The female climbed over and when she did, she dropped the daisy onto his large black nose. "Thanks, River. You really didn't have to do this." She murmured, jumping to the other side. Her head was tilted to the side as he got to his paws, resisting the urge to shake his fur.

"I had too, I couldn't let you get all wet in that muddy water!" He barked, his voice suddenly cracking. His tail was swaying back and forth as Bumble ran ahead, right now was a perfect time to shake his fur. The male shook his thick pelt, water spraying everywhere and it still got to Bumble who was farther away.

Bumble shot him a playful glare as she raised his paw above a rain puddle. "You really want to play that game, huh?" She growled, getting ready for him to walk near. Her tail was swishing back and forth even faster, her mind off the missing dogs. When she was with Rippling River, she was in a whole nother world.

"Yeah, sure, I'll play this game." He barked, bowing down, wiggling his haunches. Rippling River leaped forward, paws spread out as tumbled in front of the female. He wouldn't be able to actually touch her since, first of all she was a lady and must be respected, she also had her jam with her.

She rolled her eyes, a giggle escaping her. The female smashed her paw into the ground, water droplets flying into the air and spraying both of them. "Sucks to be you!" She howled, a smile painted onto her face. Her eyes were bright as she whipped around, taking off in another direction. Paws splashing into puddles as she ran, glancing behind her shoulders for the male who was most likely following her.

A gasp escaped Rippling River as he chased after her. Paws pounding against the ground, making the ground shake at his presence. "I'll get you back!" He barked, his voice loud and clear. "You better hide your jam when you sleep!" Rippling River called after her.

A giggle escaped her. "I'd like to see you steal my jam, Mr." She commented, still running, careful not to let her jam slip out of the pouches they had. Bumble also had to be careful to not let her plush, Red, fall out. Her tail was slowing down as a scent caught her nose.

"Oh, I could do it with my eyes closed!" He barked, skidding to a stop as he noticed her change of movement. His tail went limp and his head tilted to the side. "Everything alright?" Rippling River asked, now standing beside the female.

She lifted her nose, ignoring the male's question. It was faint, covered up by the rain, but it smelt like a dog. Panic shot through her. The smell that was twisted in with this scent was blood. Not blood that came from some prey that a dog had hunted. Real dog blood. It was fresh too.

"What's wrong?" He questioned, worry escaping him. Shivers were running down his spine now when the female wouldn't speak. "What's wrong?" The male repeated.

"Blood."

CHAPTER ELEVEN

"You're coming with us," A female barked. She was shorter than both of them. The canine appeared to be a small Beagle, no more than six months old. Her lips were curled back in a snarl as her gaze darted in between them. Her floppy ears were pinned back, her glare continuing to dart between both dogs.

The male beside her shook his head roughly. "Cliff, you don't make the rules here." He stated calmly, facing the newcomers. "Welcome to our village, what can we do for you?" The male questioned swiftly, he was also a Beagle but taller than the other. His tail was swaying back and forth, showing that he meant no harm to the newcomers.

Loud Tail stepped forward, head bowed down so the dogs could have a better look at him. "We have come to visit." He murmured, letting his tail sway back and forth. "Even though we are pack dogs, we mean no harm to you and your citizens." Loud Tail told the two Beagles, relaxing his muscles. He rolled onto the ground, revealing his most vulnerable places, his throat and his belly.

Racing Creek nodded at what his friend had said. "I am Racing Creek and he is Loud Tail." The male introduced both of them, gazing at the two in front of him. "Every word that comes out of his mouth is true." He murmured, rolling on his back like Loud Tail, to show that he means no harm.

The pup looked them up and down, confused on what they were doing. "Uhm… I'm all for playing but right now isn't the time to play…?" She barked, glancing over at her father. "Is it the time to play?" Cliff asked, her snowy white head tilting to the side as she spoke.

"No, dear it isn't the time to play." He spoke softly when he gazed down at his daughter. His tail was swaying back and forth as he brought his eyes back to the males. "By the way, they aren't trying to play, they are showing their vulnerable places to show that they mean no harm." He explained, raising his paw. "It's how pack dogs do it."

"Ohhh," The pup barked. A couple giggles escaped her as she tapped the dogs heads with her nose. "You can get up now, silly pack dogs!" She squeaked, watching them jump to their paws. A grin was splattered all over her face and her brown ears were perked as she danced around.

Racing Creek bent down and sniffed both dogs, gathering their scents. "I'm up." He barked, a chuckle escaping him. "I'm up." He repeated, a sigh escaping him. His tail was swaying back and forth as the female's adoring gaze reached his.

"You should tell me what it's like in a pack!" She squeaked, her tail swishing back and forth. Her eyes were a chestnut brown, sparkling as the sun danced around them. "Please!" Cliff squealed, hopping up and down, circling the two males. Her paws were tripping over each other, dew filled grass tickling her paw pads.

Her father let out a snort. "Cliff, I think they may want to actually visit the village and grab something to eat." He pointed out, glancing down at their grumbling bellies. The male furrowed his brow. "By the way, I'm Grove." He barked, letting his tail sway back and forth.

"Yeah, now that you say that, I'm actually starving." Racing Creek chuckled, looking down at his own belly. He wasn't the skinniest but he was still hungry all the time. Anyone would think his pack was starving him. His tail was swaying back and forth and a grin crawled onto his face. "What do you have to eat?" Racing Creek questioned, licking his chops.

"Well, we have salad, donuts, cake!" Cliff named off, jumping up and down. "Oh, yeah we also have sugar pops!" She squealed, her ears perked up as she continued to jump up and down. The female had a lot of energy, more than a pup should have. "Sugar pops are the best, they're apples covered with a bunch of sugar and drizzled in carob sauce!"

Creek glanced over at Loud Tail, his maw parted. "That sounds so good!" He barked, bowing down, his tail swishing back and forth. "Where can we get them? I need to know!" The male squealed, his eyes now focusing on Grove who let out a sigh.

"You know what, I'll go get my wife and we all can go to a restaurant." He barked, raising a paw, his black paw pads attracting sunlight. "It'll be my treat." The male murmured, turning around, looking at what was ahead of him. It was all oak trees and birch trees, no meadows shown yet.

Cliff looked at them before following her father. "It's the best place, they have sugar pops, donuts, and cake!" She named off some desserts they had with wide eyes. A bounce in every step when she followed her father. Her ears were perked up, dancing at the very least.

Grove rolled his eyes, a laugh escaping him. "There's also healthy things, like chicken, salad, and a lot of fruit." He pointed out, glancing behind him to look at the two newcomers. His tail swayed back and forth as he opened his maw to speak. "I know you guys may not know what any of that is, but I promise it's good." He reassured them.

Loud Tail nodded, furrowing his brow. His paws were making loud crunches when they hit the leaves that swayed against the ground, looking for safety. The male's tail was swishing back and forth, but much slower then Racing Creek who kept thinking about all the food he would be able to eat at the restaurant. "That does sound good." He barked, keeping his voice low so the pack dogs who were near wouldn't be able to hear.

"Agreed!" Racing Creek barked, jumping up and down just like the pup. The hunter himself was probably a pup in disguise in all honesty. His whole body was shaking when he followed the two who were leading them to the Shimmering Stars Village.

Houses came in view, they looked to be made out of clay and they all had little shutters on their windows. It was cute. They had a delightful pastel theme going on too! This was much more pretty than Racing Creek had ever imagined. Most of the houses were a pale color too with a touch of pastels.

"Woah," He gasped, looking around in awe. "Is this really your village?" Racing Creek questioned, his brown eyes wide. His maw was still parted as he glanced around, gaze darting everywhere.

"Yup!" The pup squealed, rolling in the grass that held many flowers. Her paws were fighting back at the air who had sent the wind down to her. The female's tail was uncontrollably swishing back and forth as she glimpsed at her father. "Do you think ma is gonna let us keep these two as guests?" She questioned, a smile growing on her face. "They're very nice and I think they should stay with us."

Grove nodded, shooting his gaze down to his paws. "Uh yeah," He barked, his answer delayed. The multicolored Beagle brought his gaze over to the two males. "You two are a couple, so you wouldn't mind staying in the room, right?"

Loud Tail shook his head, trying not to be sick. "We are not a couple, would never be a couple." He barked, continuing to shake his head. "We can share a room though, I'll sleep on the floor." The male barked, he stopped shaking his head when he felt a bunch of stares on his back.

Racing Creek let out a chuckle. "Am I that bad?" He questioned, leaning against the muscular male. His tail was swaying back and forth and the smile that he had on his face only grew much bigger.

"Yeah, you are that bad." Loud Tail barked, having no shame in his answer. He glanced around, his eyes meeting the citizens who glanced over to him, seeing who the newcomers were. "Are they supposed to look at me like that, Grove?" He questioned, walking away from Racing Creek.

Grove shook his head softly with a sigh. "Ignore them, they mean no harm, just curious." He barked, raising his paw

73

as he nudged his daughter to get up. His tail continued to sway back and forth as he glanced around, searching for his wife. When he did catch the eye of his wife, he lifted his caramel brown snout in a howl, hopeful to catch her attention.

"Oh, you brought newcomers I see?" She commented as she walked over to meet them. Her eyes were bright as she gazed at them and her smile the same if not brighter. The female's tail was swaying back and forth as she dipped her head to Loud Tail and Racing Creek. "Let me guess, you're bringing them to a restaurant and you want me to join you guys."

Grove parted his maw, chuckling. "How'd you know, sweetheart?" He questioned, letting his gaze meet the dirt. This was a daily thing with him and his family. Anytime there was a newcomer, he'd insist letting them in, saying it would teach their daughter manners.

She rolled her eyes. "Don't play that game with me." The female purred, bowing her head once again to the newcomers. "I'm Sadie and you two are?" She asked, her smile stunning.

"I'm Loud Tail and that goofball is Racing Creek." The Sarabi Dog introduced them, letting his tail rest on Racing Creek's back. His wrinkles were shown due to his pale tan fur. His tail was thudding against the Golden Retriever's back which he sure would think that it would annoy Racing Creek, but he still let Loud Tail keep his tail on him.

Racing Creek let a toothy grin grow on his face. "Yup, that's us!" He barked, his belly growling louder than before. His tail swayed back and forth as his back kept getting slapped by the male's tail. It brought him comfort knowing that the male trusted him enough to put his tail on him. He admired what the female looked like. She was a mostly white Beagle with brown and black spots, she also wore a pink collar.

"Beautiful names you two." She murmured, turning to face her husband. "What restaurant are we going to?" Sadie asked, her head tilting to the side. Her tail was swaying back and forth as she glanced around. Her head quickly tilted to the other side when Grove appeared puzzled.

Their pup, Cliff, jumped up, her maw parted. "Let's go to Jade's Palace!" She barked, excitement vibrating off of her. "It's the best place! Jade has a bunch of sugary stuff!" The female exclaimed, her tail swishing back and forth, faster than the speed of light.

"There's salad there too," Sadie added on. Her whole face turned too sweet to warm the minute she made eye contact with her daughter. It was like Cliff was her everything. Her floppy ears were flicking as she gave Cliff's idea a chance. "Yeah, we can go to Jade's Palace, I'm sure your father will love that place."

Grove shook his head softly. "Yeah, I will love that place." His teeth were grinding against each other as he spoke. "It'll be very fun to see Roxanne performing there." He barked, growling at the singer's name. Grove forced his tail to sway back and forth, he had to stay happy for his daughter.

"Roxanne is my favorite singer and my favorite aunt!" The female barked, tail swaying back and forth. A smile emerged on her face, ears perked up. His paws were shuffling on the ground, excitement dancing through her making it unable to stand still.

Racing Creek let out a small chuckle watching the pup dance around. "She sounds amazing." He commented, furrowing his brow. His tail was swaying back and forth and his eyes travelled over to Loud Tail. His eyes were bright when Loud Tail gazed back into them.

"She is!" Cliff barked, jumping up and down. She ran off, in the direction of the restaurant. Her tail was swishing back and forth behind her. Barks were escaping her as she got farther, not being able to stay and wait for them to actually go to the restaurant.

Grove let out a sigh. "Great, we should go catch her before she releases havoc on the dogs." He barked, fastening his pace, but not running, more like speed walking. His tail was raised as his paws slammed down on the path. There was a tiled path that led to the shops and houses, they all had paintings on them, due to stories needing to be told.

"Don't mind him, he doesn't have the best relationship with his sister." His wife had murmured, watching him start to run off for their daughter. She dipped her head, eyes focused on the tiles. "Sorry about him though, if you'd like I can tell you the stories about some of these tiles." Sadie offered, bringing her gaze up to the two taller males.

Loud Tail nodded, taking his tail off of Racing Creek. "I wouldn't mind that. Your culture seems cool compared to ours." He chuckled, following the female when she started walking after her family, but much slower. His tail was still swaying back and forth as he followed, glancing over his shoulder once in a while.

Sadie shook her head. "Everyone's culture is equal." She stated, her voice calm and collected. The female waved her paw over a pile where there was a splatter paw print, the color was a crimson red, the color of blood.

"What's that?" Racing Creek questioned, his head tilting to the side. He put his paw on the tile that Sadie was showing off. His head quickly tilted to the other side within a matter of seconds. The male's tail was swaying back and forth though, curiosity dancing around in his eyes.

"This... this is the tile that represents our founder." She barked, her voice quiet as she spoke. She took in a deep breath before telling the story. Her tail was tucked in between her stubby legs as she walked forward. Sadie parted her maw, ready to tell the story. "Our founder... well, he was one that was feared."

Loud Tail nodded slowly, letting his gaze wander as they passed shops. Some shops had plushies in the window sills while others had desserts and some even had accessories, like collars and sweaters! "Oh, that sounds interesting." He murmured, following the female, with his ears swiveled so he could hear her but not directly look at her when she was telling the story.

"It is interesting." Sadie mumbled. Her eyes were still focused on her family that was ahead of her. "He... well... he was killed shortly after he founded this village." She explained, raising her paw. "None of us usually tell this story anymore because we don't know the full story, but maybe I could take you to someone who does, tomorrow?"

Racing Creek nodded, locking his gaze on the plush store that caught his gaze. "Yeah, we'll be here tomorrow. So, uhm.... Could you get me one of those things in that window tomorrow?" He asked, pawing at the air at where the store was. "They look so cool!" He barked, jumping up and down.

Loud Tail rolled his eyes with a chuckle. He loved the Golden Retriever's personality, he always got excited over the smallest thing and he sure was a glutton. "I'm pretty sure that we're at the restaurant now." The male barked, walking in between the bickering father and daughter.

"We can go in now!" The pup barked, running into the restaurant.

Fairy Lights were hung everywhere and the tables were circular. Dogs were doing karaoke on the stage, singing their hearts away. Waiters and waitresses were delivering the customers food, having small chit chats with them before going back to work. It was a stunning view.

Racing Creek glanced around, his maw parted in awe. "Woah.." He gasped, standing in the entrance. His tail was swaying back and forth as he turned to Loud Tail. "If we stayed in the village we would have never seen this!" He barked, ears perked up and his body shaking.

Loud Tail nodded, taking in what Racing Creek had said. He was right. If they stayed in the village while chaos was thrown around, they would have never seen the beauty of this village. "You're right." He simply murmured, tail swaying back and forth.

CHAPTER TWELVE

Bumble clutched onto her plush as she gazed at Rippling River. She shook her head softly and her eyes drooped with sadness. "We still don't know where they are and what that blood scent is." She mumbled, tucking her paws closer in with her chest. The female tore her gaze away from Rippling River and watched the stars dance around the night sky.

"We'll find out soon, I promise." The Newoundland reassured the female as he stood, keeping guard. There were already two dogs guarding the camp but there was always a chance that they would need more. Better safe than sorry.

Her eyelids closed, a sigh escaping her. She dropped the plush so he was laying next to her. "What if we don't though, your pack could be in danger and we wouldn't be able to help." Bumble pointed out, continuing to point her snout up at the stars. "Hopefully, Tsunami will help us out." She murmured, lowering her snout and opening her beautiful green eyes.

"Who's... Tsunami?" He questioned, tilting his head to the side. His tail was curled around his large boulder sized paws. Rippling River opened his maw to say another thing but shut it immediately.

No answer came, only humming that Bumble was doing. It was like she was humming a lullaby she was once told, it was stunning. Her tail was swaying back and forth, rather slow compared to all the other times.

"Who is Tsunami?" He repeated, tilting his head to the other side. His paws were shuffling in the dirt as he waited for an answer. Rippling River layed down, paws stretched out as his maw opened up in a long yawn.

Bumble shook her head softly and stopped humming. "She's my sister, I have great hope that she'll find a way to help this pack out." She murmured, pointing up to a constellation in the sky that made a wave. "That's her, I just know it." The female barked, her voice soft.

"Oh..." He mumbled, not knowing what to say. "I'm sorry for your loss?" Rippling River murmured, tilting his head to the side. His tail was curled around his body, not moving when his friend had given them this news. He genuinely didn't know what to say, he never lost someone close to him before.

Bumble let out a giggle and opened her maw to say something to the male. "Don't be sorry, everything that happens is meant for a reason." She spoke, resting her head on her paws. The female continued to gaze up at the wave constellation, starting to hum once more. Bumble continued to hum the lullaby she was humming not to long ago.

"Oh, okay." Rippling River mumbled. He closed his eyes and let out a sigh. "You should get some sleep." He advised, tail swaying back and forth. His eyes opened slightly, glancing back at Bumble who was starting to snore.

"Wake up!" Bumble barked, shaking the male. Her paws were jabbing into his ribs but he still wouldn't wake up. She wiggled her haunches and leaped onto the male, gnawing at his scruff. "Wake up!" She repeated, continuing to shake him.

Rippling River pushed her off and rolled to the side. "What do you want?" He groaned, his eyes still tightly closed. His tail was swaying back and forth, slamming against the ground when it did. The council member's ears were perked up though, listening to what Bumble had to say.

"Well, I got you something but it's obvious you don't want it." She mumbled, plopping her rump down. Bumble stuck her snout in the air, trying not to smile. The female held a sunflower in her maw, she was going to give it to Rippling River but it was obvious that he didn't want to wake up. Well, it wasn't just one sunflower. She made a whole flower crown with sunflowers for him. She was currently wearing a daisy flower crown she made for herself.

Rippling River rolled over again, still not opening his eyes. "What is it?" He asked, clearly tired. His tail continued to slam against the dirt but not as loud as before. A smile was forming on his face but he kept it on the low, slowly opening his eyes.

Bumble didn't answer.

He opened his eyes fully and sat up so he could see the figure of the female. "Nice, crown you got there." Rippling River complimented, pointing out the flower crown that she was wearing. "You did a good job making it!" He barked, trying to get her to turn around and look at him.

She didn't turn around but she let the smile break through. "Thank you, but even if you compliment me, you're not getting that gift I made you." Bumble murmured, raising her snout even higher. Her tail was swaying back and forth as she gripped the flower crown much tighter.

"Aw, come on!" Rippling River whined, trying to sneak a glance at what she was holding. His ears were pressed up against his head as he still attempted to see what she was holding. Curiosity was shooting through him and he couldn't contain it. "Can I please see it?" He questioned, bowing his head. "I said please."

Bumble rolled her eyes and a giggle escaped her. "Fine, only because you said please though." She murmured, turning around. The female hopped up so she could be tall enough to place the flower crown on the male. "Like it? I made it just for you!"

"Yeah, I love it!" He barked, looking up so he could admire the beauty of it. Sunflowers were his favorite flowers and he couldn't put his paw on how Bumble knew that it was. His tail was swaying back and forth as he let his gaze drop. He stepped forward and nuzzled the stunning Weimaraner. His eyes were bright when Bumble didn't turn away from him nuzzling her. He lifted a paw and hugged her tightly, his fur hiding her.

"Stop with that lovey dovey dung and get into the den."

Gray Wind barked, an edge to her voice, more than usual though. Her fur was raised as she stormed off towards the den that they all usually meet at when something is happening.

Rippling River pulled away and raced after the female. Whatever happened got Gray Wind on edge and even though she seemed like she was on edge, she really wasn't. "Lets go, Bumble." He mumbled, paws slamming against the grass.

Both of them entered the den, meeting the bickering twins. Everything was the same, everyone was fighting over the littlest things. Nails were digging into the dirt while the sunlight danced around in the den, the mood was confusing at times.

"You all might be confused as to why I called you here." Gray Wind started, a sigh escaping her as she spoke. Her tail was curled now, but the fur on her back was still raised. Her eyes were hardened and cold as she let them drizzle over everyone. She bared her teeth at the taller dogs who were still bickering when she was speaking. "Stop it you idiots!" Gray Wind growled, pacing back and forth.

"I'm not an idiot!" Drowning Shrew snarled, clearly losing his moose scraps.

"Wait so why are we here?" Rippling River questioned, tilting his head to the side. His tail was curled around his body as he spoke, waiting for an answer.

Gray Wind dipped her head. "Me and another pack member smelled blood, dog blood, by the border." She explained, shaking her head roughly. Her head was hung low when she spoke. "But we couldn't find where the smell was coming from." Gray Wind barked, her pointed ears pressing back against her skull.

CHAPTER THIRTEEN

"How many?" The Australian Shepherd questioned, his head tilting to the side when he spoke. His docked tail was swishing back and forth. Racing Creek couldn't help but look at the piercings that climbed up his ears, there was one piercing he had that was an arrow shooting through his left ear. All of the piercings the canine had were a light gold color.

Grove counted everyone's paws, since how short he was. "We have five!" He barked, tail swaying back and forth. His paws were shuffled on the wood floor.

The male nodded, backing up. "Let me bring you to your table." He barked, walking off to the left, eyes focused on where he was going. The waiter was leading them to the table they would have. It was low to the ground and multi colored pillows. Fairy lights were also hanging from the table.

"It's very pretty!" Cliff barked, glancing back at the two pack dogs. Her whole body was shaking while her tail swished back and forth. "Don't you guys think so?" She asked, her head tilting to the side when she leaped onto a pillow, wiggling.

"It is very pretty," Loud Tail agreed. He chose a seat next to Grove, who kept glancing around anxiously. He plopped his rump down on the blue pillow, it was a bit small for him but he managed to fit. His rump continued to wiggle though trying to be comfortable in where he was sitting.

Sadie furrowed a brow, watching the large dog get stares. "You're quite the show stopper, aren't you?" She teased, a small chuckle escaping her. Her tail was swaying back and forth as she gazed at the dogs at her table. The female's ears were perked up as she listened to the chatter that was happening at different tables.

"I can't help that I'm just that handsome." He chuckled, glancing around. His nose twitched as he took in the scents that were swirling around everyone. He had never taken in these scents before but they were all good scents, some stronger than others.

Grove rolled his eyes and a smile emerged on his face. "Cliff, what are you going to get?" He asked, gazing at his daughter with interest. His tail was swaying back and forth like the others, but way faster. The male wasn't able to see his sister anywhere so he was now fine.

"I'm going to get donuts, sugar pops, cake, carob covered strawberries." She listed off all the sweets she could think of. A toothy grin painted onto her face, fangs glowing from the fairy lights that were glimmering. Her coconut brown eyes went wide and watery when she gazed up at her father. "Can I pretty pwease get them?" She questioned, pouting.

"I'm sorry but you cannot get those." Grove barked, a sigh escaping him. "At least get fruit salad and I'll ask if they can drizzle carob over it." The male murmured, dipping his head. He glanced over at his wife, looking for guidance with their little monster they created.

Sadie let out a small giggle. "You're father is right, Cliff." She murmured, a small smile emerging on her face. "I'll let you get some sugar pops too, if you do get something healthy." The female barked, with a small wink towards Grove. She was basically showing off now with her skills.

"Oki! I like ma's idea! Sorry, pa!" She barked, putting her paws onto the table. Her whole body was continuing to wiggle when she glanced over at Racing Creek and Loud Tail. "What are you guys going to get?" She asked, her head tilting to the side.

Racing Creek didn't know what there was so he tilted his head to the side. "Oh, uhm... I'll get the same thing as Cliff." He mumbled, listening to his grumbling belly. His floppy ears were pressed up against his skull as he let the scents of all the different kinds of food. "What about you, Loud Tail?"

83

"I'll get salad....?" His voice trailed off, trying to think of what salad was. "Yeah, I'll get salad." He decided, with a nod of his head. His tail was swaying back and forth yet he still struggled to get comfortable. Loud Tail glanced around, looking at all the dogs who were all different colors, shapes, and sizes. It was interesting to him, everyone in this restaurant could be the size of the pack he had or even more.

"Fruit salad or garden salad?" Grove asked with a tilt of his head.

"Uhm.... garden salad?" Loud Tail barked, his head tilting to the side. He didn't know what either of them were but he decided to choose the one that sounded more interesting. Loud Tail's rump was still wiggling all over the place, gaining a bunch of attention to those who were in the restaurant, dining.

Grove nodded with a small chuckle. "Nice choice." He commented, yawning. His teeth were doing the same that his daughter's teeth had done, they attracted the fairy lights.

An Australian Shepherd walked up to them, she wasn't the same one as before but they looked similar. They might have been brother and sister. "What can I get you all to drink today?" She questioned, her head tilting to the side. She was wearing a tux, rather formal then the others.

"We'll all get water." Sadie barked, dipping her head at the waitress.

The waitress nodded and walked off to go get what they wanted.

A whine rippled in the pup's throat and she slammed her head against the table. "Why can't I get something else? Like melon pop?" The female let her tongue loll against the table. Her ears were flopped and spread out on the table.

"You don't need that much sugar." Her mother barked, her voice almost inaudible. "You can't behave like this in restaurants either, young lady." She growled, making her voice seem firm. Her tail was curled around her body as she waited for the waitress to come back with their drinks.

Grove shook his head softly. "Your mother is right." He

calmly barked, adjusting himself so he'd be more comfortable. His ears were pinned back against his head as he spoke, glancing around. The male pawed at his ears for a few moments due to the horrible singing in the background. This was always one of the risks in this restaurant, there was always one dog who was horrible at singing.

"Ugh, finee." She groaned, continuing to slam her head down against the table. Her tail waas thudding against the ground too. Cliff was making so much noise for a pup at her age. "I wanted melon pop though!" She complained, head rolling onto the table.

Racing Creek bent his head down. "Maybe, if you stop they'll get you melon pop next time." He explained to the pup, setting one of his paws on the table. His tail swished back and forth and his paw now was up in the air. "Think about it, next time the melon pop could be better than what it would be today."

The female let her head bounce up. "I never thought about that before!" She barked, her tail now thudding much louder against the ground. Her eyes were bright when she thought about how good it could be next time she came.

"Yeah, next time they'll be amazing!" Loud Tail barked, lifting his paw up in the air and set it onto Racing Creek's head. His tail was swaying back and forth as he let his maw part in a long yawn. "Y'know this is an amazing pawrest." He barked, messing up the male's head fur.

"Can I use him as a pawrest next time?" Cliff asked, jumping up and down again. Her parents were going to hate this. Bringing Loud Tail and Racing Creek was a really good idea for them. The female's tail was swishing back and forth as her gaze darted from her mother to father. "Please!"

Sadie rolled her eyes with a small giggle. "Maybe, tomorrow." She murmured, gazing at Loud Tail with warmth and sweetness, it would never change. Even if she felt a different way she'd have to be the perfect dog that everyone thought of her to be.

"Oh, oki!" She barked, slamming her paws onto the table. "When is dinner going to come?" The female whined, her eyes growing restless as they waited.

There were two dogs that came to the table this time, it was the Aussie siblings. One had the plates while the other took them off. "May you enjoy your meal." The male barked, his snout raised with a wide smile. His tail was swaying back as he made eye contact with Racing Creek.

"We will!" Cliff barked, already digging into her meal. Her whole snout was covered in carob sauce but right when someone mentioned it, she licked her chops getting rid of it all, well most of it. Her tail was swaying back and forth and she giggled when there was a strawberry on her nose. "Look, there's a strawberry on my nose!" She barked, focusing her gaze on it.

"Aren't you going to eat it?" Her father asked, threatening to snatch it. "If you don't I'll gladly take it." He teased, a smile emerged on his face. His tail was swishing back and forth as he watched his daughter turn away and eat the strawberry.

Cliff shook her head softly. "You can't eat it anymore!" She barked, digging her face into her salad once again. Her snout was covered in juices from the fruit.

Racing Creek poked the salad with his nail and sniffed at it. It smelt different from all the other things he had eaten before. He ate a pawful of the berries, a mixture of raspberries, strawberries, and blueberries. It was good, but not as good as what he usually got out in the wild.

"How are you liking it?" Loud Tail questioned, furrowing his brows as he looked at Racing Creek. His tail was swaying back and forth as he kept eating mouthfuls of his salad within seconds. The male's rump still wiggled from time to time but it looked as if he had gotten way more comfortable.

"It's not too bad." Racing Creek answered, still poking some parts of it with his nail.

They all exited the restaurant, all of their bellies full

with food. Cliff wouldn't stop burping while Sadie scolded her, telling her that young ladies should have manners. Tails were swishing back and forth an dGrove complained about the singing.

All of the dogs were on their way to their way to the couple's house when Racing Creek opened his maw to ask a question. "Do you guys know a Daisy by any chance?" He asked, his head tilting to the side. This was his one and only chance to find out if she was in this village.

Grove nodded. "Uh, yeah, she works at the bakery, why?" He asked, his head now tilting to the side. His tail stopped swaying back and forth when he waited for an answer.

"I'm her son." He answered, closing his eyes. Racing Creek shook his head softly. "How far away is your house?" The male asked, his voice now much more quiet than before. His tail was still swaying back and forth.

Sadie lifted her head and let out a bark. "We're here already!" She announced, walking into the building. It was one of the more pastel looking houses. There were flowers all over the building adding an aesthetically pleasing look to it.

"I really like this place of yours." Loud Tail complimented the house when he followed the female in. It was very spacious with toys thrown around. He looked behind him and there was a welcoming mat at the door. He had never been in a real house before and it was so cozy.

Grove stifled a laugh. "Thanks, I'll lead you to yours and Racing Creek's room." He offered, forming a smile on his face.

CHAPTER FOURTEEN

Bumble paced back and forth, her head hung low. "What are we going to do?" She barked, her voice muffled. Her heart was pounding against her chest as she glanced behind her. The female's tail was tucked in between her legs and she lifted her snout to howl.

"Nothing," A voice murmured. The voice was eerie and like nothing she ever heard. "I don't even know why you joined this pathetic pack I'm trying to get rid of." She snarled, tail swaying back and forth. Her eyes were focused on Bumble yet Bumble was unable to see her.

"I didn't join it," The female stated. Her fur started to raise, both the fur on her back and her tail. "I'm only visiting." She growled, her gaze darting around. Bumble's tail was raised and her eyes were narrowed. She wouldn't let some dog get in her business. Her paw steps made no sound when she crept low, playing the same game that the other, unknown, dog was playing.

The female that was well hidden cackled. "Oh my dog, poor, poor, *Bumble.*" She snarled, ear tufts poking out from the surrounding darkness. "Can't realize that love makes you stay and love makes you regret." Her voice grew darker and louder as the figure approached.

"What do you mean?" She questioned, backing up till she slammed into a monstrous sized tree. Her tail was now tucked and her gaze darted around. She didn't like this. She didn't like this at all. "What do you mean?" Bumble repeated, her voice sharp and her teeth bared.

"You really don't know what I mean?" The female

laughed, her laugh was sickening, it could make anyone's bones shiver. The ear tufts of her still shown in the moonlight, they were a creamy brown color. "You're falling for Rippling River, darling. Yet, one day he won't be there." Her voice was somehow calm and collected, like she knew just what to say.

"How do you know his name?" Bumble asked, trying to back up even more but failing. The fur on her tail and the fur on her back. Her eyes continued to dart around, glowing in the darkness.

"Oh, just ask him about *Sora*." She growled and the female launched at her but was knocked off by an unknown force. Her blood covered snout twisted up in disgust as she saw a ghostly figure. Water was pouring down on the female, who she could not see.

Her maw parted, confusion swarming around her like angry bees. That's when she saw glowing blue eyes. Bumble's whole body started to shake and her eyes went wide. It was her sister. It was Tsunami. "W-what…?" Her voice trailed off as she stared into the darkness. "Tsunami…?"

The female parted her maw and whispered. "Run." Her figure was beautiful, agile with waves at her paws. She couldn't help but wonder what happened if her sister wasn't there.

She woke up in the shaman's den, her paws stinging. "What happened…?" Bumble asked, wincing as pain shot through her body. The female's eyes were tightly closed as she started to wobble, attempting to stand up. She instantly fell to the ground and a growl ran through her throat.

"I don't know," Jagged Paw murmured. He shook his head, searching for herbs that he would need. "Ancient Willow found you out in the forest, passed out and bleeding." The male told the female, tail raised as he limped throughout the den. Jagged Paw opened his maw to ask a question but shut it. He quickly opened it again, realizing that there had to be some hope. "Do you remember anything that happened?"

She remembered the glowing eyes but what they were

she was unsure of. The female shook her head slowly, laying it against the stone cold ground. "I... no... I don't remember anything that happened." Bumble told him, her eyes flickering open. She looked up at the roof of the den and it had paintings on it, like it was telling some unknown story.

He nodded at what she said and let a small chuckle escape him as she gazed up at the roof of the den. "Oh, so you're looking at that?" Jagged Paw asked, not expecting an answer. He sighed, sitting next to the female. "I really don't know what it came from, I always asked Cleared Sky but she never told me where or why it was there." He shook his head softly, bowing his head.

"Oh," She mumbled. The female pointed to one with multiple paw prints and then a wave hovering above them, threatening to wash them out. "Maybe that one is when the pack maybe got driven out or there was a flood?" She guessed, her head tilting to the side. The female was pretty good at telling stories with pictures, but sometimes if she didn't know the place well it was much harder for her.

"Maybe..." Jagged Paw's voice trailed off when he took Bumble's idea about it into thought. "Y'know, you might be right about that one." He murmured, tail swaying back and forth. The fur on his head was all wet due to the droplets falling from the roof of the den. "What do you think about that one?" He questioned, pointing to where there was a face of a dog but the eyes were blacked out. Red berry juice was splattered all over it too.

She tilted her head, not sure what it could mean. "I actually don't know, are there any blind dogs in this pack?" The female questioned, wincing again from the pain that shot through her. She lifted her paws and looked at the cobwebs that were covering them along with leaves mixed in with them.

"Yeah, Cleared Sky and Birch." He mumbled, continuing to study the painting. His head tilted to the side and he lifted his good paw to touch it, feeling the movement of the dried paint. "These paintings are older then Birch though." The male mumbled, setting his paw down so he wouldn't have to balance on his hind legs.

"Oh, okay. They're not older than Cleared Sky though, am I right?" She asked, her head tilting to the side. The female was still lying on the ground but she still wanted to get up. If she did stand though, she'd fall to the ground due to her injuries on her paw pads.

Jagged Paw nodded, still gazing up at the roof. "Yeah... maybe this is about her." He decided, fidgeting with stray pebbles that lay on the ground. His tail was curled around his body as his eyes narrowed. "She was never that open about her backstory." He pointed out, gaze darting around. "So, maybe the reason why she wouldn't tell me about these paintings... maybe she made these to track the history in the pack."

"Maybe." She murmured, continuing to check on her paw pads. The female's maw parted in a yawn and she curled up in a ball. Her eyes were closing, tempted to try to flicker open but they were too heavy for her to hold up. She soon fell into a deep sleep.

She woke up to the sound of yelling. The scent of panic was running throughout the pack. What was happening? Did another murder happen or was a festival happening? "What's happening?" She asked, seeing that Cleared Sky was sitting in front of her.

"Squawking Parrot gave birth last night when you were sleeping, I really don't know how you slept through it though." She murmured, lifting her snout. "But... they're stolen now." Her voice grew rough, terrified of what could happen. Cleared Sky's tail was curled over her body and her eyes seemed darkened, like she knew what happened.

Bumble attempted to stand up but fell to the ground. "What...." Her voice trailed off as shock ran through her. "No..." The female's voice trailed off once again, not believing what happened. "Who.... Who did this?" She questioned, not expecting an answer.

"I.... I can't say... but they'll come back... I know they

will... both the pups and the dog." Cleared Sky mumbled, her eyes wide and tearing up. She lifted her paws up to the air. "The darkness will end up taking everything, there's nothing that will be able to stop it unless we all come together."

CHAPTER FIFTEEN

Grove led, both Loud Tail and Racing Creek, to the bakery and dipped his head. "Good luck, we'll be back at the house if you need us." He murmured, turning around. His tail was swaying back and forth and the silver tag that hung from his collar swirled around from the wind. Grove's ears were perked up and his paws the slightest thud against the stone tiles.

Racing Creek bowed his head with a small chuckle. "We won't be needing luck, I'm related to Daisy after all." He barked, walking into the bakery, his head held high. His tail was swaying back and forth, but not because he wanted it to sway back and forth. He dreaded this day. His mother was a traitor to this pack and would always be one.

Loud Tail followed after Racing Creek, his eyes focused on the ground. He felt stares reach him, it was never like this in the pack, he may be really big but no one paid attention to that. Maybe they were looking at him like this because he didn't live here but wouldn't they look at Racing Creek the same way. "Uh..."

Racing Creek let out a sigh, closing his eyes. "Is there a Daisy here? Cream furred Golden Retriever?" He asked, letting his gaze drizzle over the bakery, it has never been this cold. His ears were pressed against his skull as a canine stepped forward.

"Yes, what do you need me for?" She wore a baby blue collar and a pastel rainbow tux. Her fur was neatly cleaned, no stray strands of fur poking out. The female betrayed the pack for this luxury. One could say Racing Creek and Loud Tail were betraying the pack for going here but at least they were actually trying to help out the pack.

A chuckle rippled in Racing Creek's throat as he stepped forward. "Oh, I just came to son and mother time." He growled, raising his paw. "I never really did get that because you left me and my sister!" The male's snout twisted into a snarl, fangs glistening as the sunlight danced around the bakery. His tail was raised as he waited for his mother's response. She just stood there though.

Loud Tail walked over toward Racing Creek standing over him and looking down at the female retriever. His tail was raised and the stares that he got only increased. "It will look really bad on your reputation if you don't answer your son, Miss. Daisy."

"I didn't think you'd find me." She murmured, sighing. "I'm sorry I left you, but I had no choice." The female explained, backing up, overwhelmed by the large male. Her tail was swaying back and forth slowly when she closed her eyes. "You know what? We can go to my house and talk this over." She mumbled, glancing around at the stares that they were getting. Daisy lived in a small village so this would be one of the latest gossips that went around, but then another would come and all would be fine.

"Okay," Racing Creek mumbled. He crawled out from underneath the large male and followed his mother out of the bakery. Would this really be worth his time? Was what he was looking for even here The patch of fur he found on the bus was cream and his mother's pelt was a creamy brown but what if he was wrong? This could be bad. "Where is your house?" He questioned, shaking his head softly.

"It's not too far actually." The female replied, a small smile emerging on her face. "Anyways, so uhm how did you find out that I was going to be at the bakery?" She asked, her head tilting to the side. Her creamy fur was swaying back and forth in the wind sometimes being violently tugged.

"Grove and Sadie told us you'd be there." Racing Creek mumbled, no emotion swirling around his voice. He couldn't show his mother what he was feeling. She didn't deserve to know anything about him, she left him and his sister within a heartbeat. Not thinning about how her actions could affect the pack. "They're actually really nice and seem like amazing parents to Cliff, *unlike you*." He growled the last part, his voice cold and twisted when he spoke to her.

Daisy met Racing Creek's eyes, she was calm and collected even though her son acted so cold to her. "I was young and made mistakes." She growled, her paw slammed down against the ground. "If I brought you and Willow here, you would have to restart your lives like I did!" Daisy pointed out, frozen in place. "Would you really want that, Creek?"

"It's actually *Racing Creek* now and Willow is *Ancient Willow*." Loud Tail snarled, rolling his eyes. "If you actually stayed with your pups, you'd know that." He barked, raising his front paw to gently scrape the spine of Daisy. Why couldn't she accept that she was a terrible parent and still was?

Daisy faced Loud Tail, tears forming in her eyes. "I couldn't stay with them, I was chased out!" She snarled, teeth bared at the much taller male. Her tail was raised along with the fur on her back and tail. "I didn't want to tell Racing Creek this but you two keep accusing me of being a terrible parent! Maybe I was but you two are being terrible dogs!" Her voice grew louder and now dogs that were passing grabbed a quick glimpse of them but they quickly looked away.

Racing Creek got up in the female's face. "Oh, so how are we supposed to believe that you out of all dogs were chased out of the pack?" He growled, his fur standing on edge. "You were the alpha's favorite, Singing Crow's favorite." The male added on shortly after, his tail not daring to swing back and forth. "Besides, everyone told me that you had to leave. Leave on your free will."

"Well, I didn't leave on my free will!" She growled, falling to the ground due to the pressure that was being put on her. Tears were crawling down her face, soaking her cheeks.

A beautiful red and white Siberian Husky ran forward, licking the tears off her wife. "What are you two rascals doing!?"

The female growled, fur raised as her gaze darted from the two males. Her tail was raised and her pointed ears were pinned back against her fragile skull. "Can't you two leave her alone!"

Racing Creek shook his head softly. "No, I will not leave my mother alone. I'm searching for answers that she hid from me for a year!" He snarled, his teeth were shiny but they all had a yellow tint to them. His tail was raised as he gazed at the female. "Who are you supposed to be? My long lost aunt?" He mocked, rolling his eyes. Racing Creek really wasn't in the mood for all of this.

"I'm her wife," The female growled. She wore a large black vest that had a bold white text on it, there was also a gold badge on it. "Also, you're not acting like a son should act. It's obvious that you haven't been taught manners." The sheriff added on, her ears slowly pointing back up.

Daisy stood back up, facing the two males. "Huckleberry, it's fine. You know that I get overwhelmed quickly. Her eyes were focused on Racing Creek though, they were filled with something... regret... maybe. "Look, I'm sorry I can't tell you why I got chased out." She murmured, dipping her head. "Please... please forgive me." Daisy begged, her eyes matching Racing Creek's.

"I... I don't know." His voice wasn't a growl anymore, more sympathetic like he realized what he had caused. "I'm sorry for growling at you, that wasn't very nice of me." The male whipped his head around and stuffed it into Loud Tail's fur. "I'm sorry ma." He repeated, he couldn't believe what he had just done. Even if Daisy was a terrible mother, he should still be a good dog and being a good dog is forgiving those who hurt you. "I... forgive you." He choked out, closing his eyes tightly.

Loud Tail pulled him tighter and put a paw on his back. He couldn't stand to see Racing Creek like this. "It's going to be okay." The male whispered, pulling him in. "It will be okay." He repeated softly, he didn't care that he'd probably get stares. He didn't want to see Racing Creek like this, it hurt him.

The sheriff rolled her eyes at what was happening. "Okay,

so basically I'm a mom now?" She asked Daisy, her head tilting to the side and her nose scrunched up. When she didn't get an answer soon enough for her liking, she furrowed her brow and tapped his wife.

"Yeah, I guess you are." Daisy barked, glancing around. "Do you mind that?" She questioned, gazing into her wife's ice blue eyes. Her head was tilted to the side and her ears flopped over. She looked adorable when she did that, she was really just like Racing Creek. Their personalities were similar and their habits were too.

"I really don't mind, but if he keeps up with this behavior I will mind." She growled, her head lowered as she gazed at the male.

Loud Tail rolled his eyes once again at this family stuff. "Well, if you all have this figured out maybe you guys can chat and have family time, not where everyone is watching?" He suggested, waving his paw to make his point. Many dogs were watching them. Oh, moondancer, this family was confusing.

"Yeah, yeah." Daisy murmured, glancing around at the dogs who were watching. Her ears were pressed up against her skull as she lowered her gaze.

CHAPTER SIXTEEN

It's been a few days since the incident. The pups have been returned safely, suckling at their mother's belly. Cleared Sky has been quiet, no longer wanting to talk. Things have caused panic ever since. If this was the same dog that murdered the other two dogs they were in danger. A lot of danger. This dog was more capable than anyone thought they could be.

Bumble already had a clue on who it was, due to that horrific dream she had. Was it a dream though? She did end up in the shaman's den with injured paws. Was Tsunami really there, she couldn't have been, it was impossible. *It was impossible.*

She remembered the female's voice loud and clear, it was innocent like, like she was a younger dog. Why would a younger dog do this though? She had so much to live for and now she's doing this with her life.

Maybe, Bumble could get a better glance of the female and find out who it is once in for all. She already knew the name and she already knew that she had creamy brown fur. Her name was Sora. Sora told her to ask Rippling River about her, did he do anything to upset the male?

Sora also said that she was falling in love but that was such a lie. She had to keep travelling meaning she wouldn't be able to fall in love. After all this was solved she would start travelling again but things got interesting yet scary at the same time. There was no way that she was going to leave when all this was happening.

Racing Creek and Loud Tail were still missing too. Some made jokes that Racing Creek convinced Loud Tail to go live in the village with him, just like Racing Creek's mother had done once. Bumble wouldn't believe it but there was really no way in proving it was true or false.

Her paws shuffled around in the dirt, a sigh escaping her. No one was coming up to her to ask if she wanted to go on a patrol of any kind. It was like they were purposely ignoring her. Rippling River was too busy to come around and say hello. He was a council member, why did she think that he would ever stick around to be great friends, he had greater responsibilities, more important responsibilities.

Maybe it was time that she found new friends within this pack. Who would want to be friends with a traveller like her though? Maybe Muddy Ears would like to be friends, she seemed rather friendly. In fact she was laying down across camp, hiding from the overwhelming sun that burned everything in its path.

The female stood up, bandages still wrapped around her paws. It was for the better that way. Her movements were slower than before since it felt like there were thorns stabbing into her paw pads each time she took a step forward. Her ears were perked up and her tail was swaying back and forth.

The Pitbull lifted her head up as Bumble approached. "Hey, girly! How are you doing?" The female asked, bending her head down to get another bite of the mouse she was eating. She wore a necklace made out of tulips and it was really pretty, well in Bumble's opinion it was.

"Oh! I've been doing well I guess." Bumble barked, plopping her rump down, admiring the female's beauty. "What about you?" The female tilted her head to the side, still wearing the daisy crown she had made. Was Rippling River still wearing the sunflower one or did he ditch it?

She shook her head softly, finishing up the last of her meal. "I've been fine, so don't worry about me." Muddy ears murmured, scratching her ear with her hind leg. Her eyes travelled over to where Rippling River was talking to Gray Wind. "What happened to you and your man talking? Y'all haven't been talking for at least three days now."

Bumble dipped her head, her eyes growing sad. "He's too

busy doing his *important* responsibilities to even care about his friend anymore, I guess." She mumbled, forcing her tail to sway back and forth. She made her ears perk up and she lifted her gaze. "Would you like to try some of my *world famous* jam?" Bumble barked, with a giggle escaping her.

"Sure!" The female barked, rolling her eyes at the sarcasm that Bumble had. Her tail was swaying back and forth and she furrowed her brow. "You don't have it on you, what a rare sight!" She chuckled, rolling to her side. Her tongue was lolled and her ears flopped over.

The female shook her head softly and let out a small chuckle. "Let me go get it." She murmured, turning away from the white female. Bumble glanced over her shoulder though. "What kind of jam would you like?" She questioned, starting to trot off.

"Uhm, apple please!" She called back, Muddy Ears didn't care what jam she got since she never tried it. Her tail was swaying back and forth as she watched the female go get the jam she wanted. Bumble was more chill then the pack brought her out to be.

Bumble trotted back over to where her friend sat, her head held high. She was carrying the jar of jam in her maw. Tail swaying back and forth as her paws made the smallest thud against the ground. "Here you go!" She barked, setting the jar on the ground.

"Is it good?" Muddy Ears questioned, her head tilting to the side. She wasn't doubting it but she was still unsure about it. It could taste disgusting and she wouldn't be able to get it out of her mouth. Her tail was swaying back and forth as Bumble uncrewed the lid from it and set the cloth gently on the grass.

Bumble shook her head and rolled her eyes. "No, it's absolutely disgusting." She barked, handing the jar over to the more muscular female. The female opened her maw to say something but closed it again, the process repeated. "Do you have a uh leaf I could use?"

Muddy Ears let out a giggle and grabbed one of the leaves

that were scattered around. "Here ya go *Miss. Jam*." She teased, a smirk crawling up her face. Her tail was flicking side to side as she waited for Bumble to respond to her new nickname she had made.

"I like the new nickname I got." She replied with a laugh escaping her. Bumble spread out the jam on the leaf and passed it over to Muddy Ears. Her tail was swaying back and forth as she eagerly waited for the female to try what she had made from scratch.

The female licked it up, her nose scrunched up. She passed it back, her tongue sticking out. "Sorry, but it isn't my favorite." Muddy Ears apologized, setting her head on her paws. Her ears were pinned back, not wanting to hurt Bumble's feelings.

Bumble still let a smile grow on her face with that feed-back. "Thank you for being honest with me!" She barked, taking back the jam. Her tail was swaying back and forth as she gazed into the honey brown eyes that belonged to the stunning Pit-bull.

"You're welcome, I'm sorry again but I'd rather stick to meat." She chuckled, shaking her head softly. Her tail was sway-ing back and forth as she met the female's gaze. They both stared into each other's eyes for at a least a minute.

"You two are needed on a border patrol." Rippling River barked, his voice emotionless as he stared at them. If you looked close enough in his eyes though, there was the smallest cloud of jealousy floating around it. His tail was raised and his eyes were narrowed. "I'll be leading this patrol."

Muddy Ears nodded, jumping to her paws. "What border will we be patrolling?" She asked, her head tilting to the side as the male glared at her.

"North." He answered, his voice cold.

A bunch of bickering broke out between Rippling River and Muddy Ears due to Rippling River being overly jealous. It was like this the whole walk there. Paws slamming against the ground and dirt being thrown, along with pebbles. Eventually, they did get there but the arguing and bickering never did stop.

"Do you smell that?" Muddy Ears asked, glancing around. Her eyes scanned the clearing they were in, sometimes climbing up the tall trees that surrounded everyone. Soil under her paws was slowly breaking as she dug her nails deep into it.

Rippling River rolled his eyes. "What?" He asked, tilting his head to the side. His ears were pressed up against his head as he glared at Muddy Ears, his nose twitching. What did she smell? There was nothing out of the ordinary so it couldn't be that important.

"An idiot." She whispered, trying not to burst out with laughter. Muddy Ears fell to the ground, rolling around, Her ears were pressed up against her skull as she cackled. Her tail was swishing back and forth as she did so. Bumble had to admit though, all this was funny.

Rippling River plopped his rump down with a scoff. "That's not funny at all." He growled, his snout twisted in a snarl. His tail was raised and his fur was raised along his spine down to the very tip of his tail. Surprisingly, he still wore the sunflower crown that Bumble had made him.

"You gotta admit it River, it was pretty funny." Bumble barked, tapping him on the nose. A giggle escaped her as she rolled around in the grass, leaving her scent near the territory marker. Her tail was swishing back and forth as grass hooked onto the pads of her paws.

Rippling River closed his eyes, letting out a sigh. "Don't call me River again." He growled, facing away from the females. "For the record, it will never be funny."

"Whatever, I guess." Bumble mumbled, turning away. She'd leave him alone, maybe she'd just escape the pack for a while. Maybe she'd meet Sora again.

CHAPTER SEVENTEEN

"Daisy... I need your help..." Racing Creek barked, a sigh escaping him. He didn't like asking for help but he needed it. She might know what's been happening. Dear, Orion, please say no one else got hurt. If he had too he'd cry out at the starry night sky, praying to the gods and goddesses up above.

Loud Tail sat beside him, sitting on an extra large cushion this time. He knew what Racing Creek was going to ask. They needed to go back home soon but would they accept them again? After all, they could say that they were escaping the pack for a pampered life, away from death and destruction.

She tilted her head, her floppy ears flopping over. "With what?" The female questioned, furrowing her brow. It really depended what it was, if it was really bad she was likely to cower out of it. Her tail was swaying back and forth rather slowly.

"The pack is in danger." He barked, fur slowly raising on his spine. His paws were shuffling against the hardwood floor as he stared at his mother. Racing Creek's eyes were desperate. She could know something they didn't know. Any information was useful.

Daisy closed her eyes, taking in a deep breath. "What do you mean by that?" Sho shook her head softly, trying to understand what he was trying to get at. Her eyes were darkened yet still bright, trying to keep hopeful for the pack. All she knew was that the pack was in danger.

"Dogs... they're dying... they're being killed." Creek mumbled, his head lowered to the ground. His tail was curled around his body. The male's eyes were down on the ground, not ready to look in the eye of Daisy, well Warm Daisy if she decides to come back to the pack to help out.

She shook her head softly, bringing her gaze over to her wife. "We'll try to help everyone out, it's the best I could do after all." The female decided, a small smirk crawling onto her face. She flicked her tail to the side when she jumped to her paws. "Hey, honey?" The female called out, her ears twitching.

"Yeah?" The Siberian Husky tilted her head to the side, suspicion dancing around in her eyes. "What do you want?" She questioned, rolling her eyes. The female was cutting up fruits but she had to stop to listen to the female. Her brows were furrowing when Daisy didn't answer her. "What do you want?" She repeated.

Daisy made her eyes go wide and her tail swayed back and forth. "Well, you see..."

A few hours passed by, Daisy and Huckleberry saying bye to their loved ones. Racing Creek and Loud Tail had already said their goodbyes to the family that brought them into this village. This was the day that they would finally venture back to the pack. Would they accept them again?

They all entered the redwood forest, prey scents running around them.

Huckleberry glanced around, still wearing her police vest and badge. Daisy just knew that she would end up bossing everyone around if they got in fights. It's what police did in the village so it would be a natural instinct for her.

Racing Creek danced around, his nose placed in the air. "It's wonderful to be back here!" He howled, his ears perked up. "I couldn't imagine staying in that crowded village any longer!" The male barked, his voice loud and clear. His paws made loud thuds against the ground as he wiggled his haunches. He smelled rabbit and he wasn't going to let it get away. Not this time!

Loud Tail furrowed his brow and whispered something into Daisy's ear. He was watching Racing Creek carefully and they both let out a small chuckle. Both of their tails were swaying back and forth while Huckleberry scouted out the area.

Racing Creek dropped down and wiggled his haunches once again. His eyes were narrowed as he gazed at what was in front of him. If he could catch this rabbit, his pack will end up being happy for his return. Especially, since he brought back a rabbit. His tail stood out like a broken branch but that was what it was supposed to look like, he wouldn't scare off prey like this.

The rabbit was near. He could smell it, the scent got stronger every time he stepped closer. His nose was scrunched up as he stalked forward. The male needed to catch it. His paw steps grew much quieter and he glanced around, searching for an area that would be an escape route for the rabbit.

The sun was shining down on them, no clouds in the air. It made Racing Creek's dark ginger pelt shimmer, sparkles slow dancing on it. The sunlight didn't burn him one bit though like all the other times, it had mercy this time around, maybe the sun god was happy with his actions.

A flash of brown and black fur met the corner of Racing Creek's eye. He wiggled his haunches once again and leaped forward. His paws slammed down in the dirt, kicking up dust as he ran off, chasing his prey. He would get it. The male started to run the other direction, planning to cut off the rabbit's exit.

A smirk was painted onto his face and his tongue threatened to slide out. His tail was now swaying back and forth, the wind dancing through his pelt.

The rabbit skidded to a stop as it realized what the canine had done. It was way too late though. Racing Creek swiped his maw down and sunk his teeth into the rabbits throat. He shook it violently afterwards, making sure it was dead and that he wasn't bringing back alive prey.

He trotted back to the others who were now rolling on the ground, cackling. Of course. There were two other dogs there too. Bumble and Muddy Ears.

"I brought pre-" Racing Creek started to say something but Bumble ran over to him and jumped on him. She was licking him all over in the face, her tail swishing back and forth, faster then he'd ever seen before. He pushed her off with a laugh rippling in his throat.

"I've missed you!" She barked, laying her head on his back. "Don't do that again, you big dummy!" Bumble growled, closing her eyes as a smirk emerged on her face. "Or should I say short dummy?" She taunted, running off so he wouldn't be able to catch her.

Racing Creek let his gaze dart between the four dogs. "Watch this rabbit or better yet bring it to camp." He ordered, but right after he raced after the female. His legs were shorter then Bumble's but he could still run swiftly. It would just be a little issue trying to catch up to the female. His tail was swishing back and forth as his tongue slid out of his mouth, drool slamming down onto the grass.

Bumble glanced over her shoulder and stuck her tongue out. "Good luck with catching me, shorty!" She called out, sliding into a bush where he wouldn't even think of looking. The tip of her tail was poking out of the berry bush, thorns fighting to go on a ride.

He rolled his eyes with a scoff. "Well, at least I'm not tall like you!" The male growled, creeping around. His nose was stuck up into the air, searching for the smell of Bumble. Racing Creek's tail was swaying back and forth as he continued to prowl.

"Having trouble finding me?" Bumble barked, jumping out of the bush, shaking her pelt. Her tail was raised, swishing back and forth. The female's eyes were a bright amber, glowing bright as she made contact with Racing Creek. Bumble hopped over a few twigs and ran in the direction of camp.

Racing Creek chuckled and raised his paw. "As if." The male leaped forward, nails digging into the soil. He would catch up to her and he would get her back for licking him. His tail continued to swish back and forth while his paws were threatening to slip on some stray mud.

She glanced back at him before exiting the camp. "Slippin' on mud, huh?" Bumble teased, swirling around. Her tail was whacking the air and her head was raised high. The female glanced around at the dogs who were staring, but they weren't staring at her.

Racing Creek shrunk down when he saw everyone sending stares into his back. *The others aren't here yet?* He asked in his head, expecting no one but himself to answer. His tail was tucked in between his quivering legs as he nervously chuckled. "I brought a rabbit!" Racing Creek blurted out.

Gray Wind walked over to where Racing Creek was, furrowing her brows. Her tail was swishing back and forth but she decided she wanted the most serious demeanor. "Where is this so called rabbit you brought?" She questioned, her ears swiveling to a side.

A warm voice called out, shaking the tiniest bit. "I have it." Daisy announced, walking into the camp. She also held a mole. Her tail was raised as her gaze flickered over her. Whispers were dancing around the camp, all about her. She dropped the prey on the ground, stepping back, showing that she meant no harm.

"Welcome back, Warm Daisy." Scrawny Raven growled, glancing down at the prey she brought with pure disgust. Her docked tail was raised as she glared at the female. "I assume the scrawny mole is yours? You really think that we'd eat that?" She questioned, her snout twisted.

Warm Daisy raised her head, her gaze calm and collected once again. She would break but not yet. She couldn't break in front of the whole pack. "Didn't you always say, prey was prey, no matter what?" The female questioned, tilting her head to the side. Her tail was also now raised.

Her gaze hardened. "Yeah and that was in the past." She growled, staring right into the eyes of Warm Daisy. Tail still raised and twitching.

"What I did was in the past too, then?" Warm Daisy shot back, standing still. The pack's gaze was switching from Scrawny Raven's and Warm Daisy's. What she had done must have been really bad.

No answer came.

Muddy ears bounced in and she knocked over the Golden Retriever when she entered the camp. Her tail was swaying back and forth as she gazed around at everyone. The female's eyes were also quite bright and excited. "Welcome back, girly!" She howled, her nose twitching as a droplet continued to lay down on it.

Loud Tail nodded, furrowing his brow. "Yeah, welcome back Warm Daisy!" He barked, joining the howl that Muddy Ears had made. His tail was swaying back and forth as his snout was raised high, the sun god looking down at him in pride.

Creek lifted his snout in a howl too, his was stunning, yet cracking at the smallest bits. His tail was swaying back and forth as others joined them. Were they really going to accept her that easy? Maybe, they knew they were all in danger. Huckleberry, still wasn't here and when she came some would throw a miniature tantrum about it.

Soon the whole pack was howling except the alphas, especially Singing Crow who was glancing down at her paws. Her tail was curled around her body as she avoided eye contact with everyone.

Huckleberry trotted in, a scroll stuffed into her maw. "Some dog wanted me to give you this." She barked, her head tilting to the side. "She said that y'all should be scared or something." The female barked, blood splattered all over her snout. "I didn't let her get away with the threat though!"

CHAPTER EIGHTEEN

Bumble watched as the reactions to the new dog strolled in. Some were curious while others were furious. Her head was tilted to the side, she knew the dog a little bit only because Muddy Ears found her and she ended up joining. The female seemed really nice so she wasn't sure why they weren't accepting.

Scrawny Raven's snout twisted in a snarl. "Quiet!" She growled, letting her gaze rest on Huckleberry. She closed her darkened brown eyes for a moment, breathing in the scents that the new dogs brought into their camp. Her paws steps were slamming down against the dew filled grass. The female's eyes were wide as she approached the blood stained husky. "May I have that scroll?" She questioned, tilting her head to the side.

Huckleberry nodded, spitting the scroll out. The scroll itself was torn and had blood splattered all over it. Her tail was raised yet patches of fur were missing from it and blood was welling from those patches of skin. The female also had blood running down her shoulder but no serious injuries due to the vest she was wearing, it protected her vulnerable spots, her neck and belly.

The female spread it out against the ground and opened her maw to read it out loud.

DEAR TUMBLING STONES PACK.
UNKNOWN.
We all know that you're going to run out of pack members. Well soon. Why not give it up and bring your pampered rumps somewhere else. Y'all don't deserve to be in this forest. Horrific beast I tell

you. That's what you are. Horrific beast. Hunting down all the prey till none is left. Your pack isn't the only one who lives in this forest. I do too. My coyote friends do too. We're out for revenge. I have already met some of your foolish pack members. Some were clever but oh well, I've met two of them, well they aren't even a part of your pack I assume. Hmmm, what's her name? Bumble? Oh and that little pup, Chase I think it was. Oh and that little elder, I did you guys a favor. I knew how much all of you hated him, an annoying little rat in all honesty.

Just wanted to tell you all to be careful, I have spies on the inside. More of your dogs will get killed if you don't learn to be smart and move to one of those horrible villages near you. All of you would be much better there, no losing poor pups to my coyote friends when they're hungry. What a good deal?

Maybe, if you do decide to leave for a village. Bring me a scroll where the owl sleeps and mice gather. I will reveal myself there. But, if you don't do this. Bye, bye, little doggies.

Love you all, xoxo

Dogs glanced around, whimpers rippling in their throats. Some turned to Bumble, suspicion and betrayal swirling around in their eyes. Tails were tucked between quivering legs and pups slid into the nursery, poking their little heads out. Ears were pressed up against delicate skulls.

Singing Crow raised her snout, eyes scanning the canines that were in the pack. "There's no need to worry about anything." She announced, her ears perked up. "No one is going to get hurt, we'll deal with this." The female barked, raising her paw. Then, she slammed her paw down on the scroll, blood smearing onto her paw pad. Her tail was raised, letting out yet another howl.

Scrawny Raven stood next to her mate, glossy pelt attracting the sunlight, soon to be moonlight. "Singing Crow is right." She barked, lowering her gaze down to the ground. "Our ancestors won't let our pack be driven out!" The female howled, her snout raised to the sun. Her tail was swaying back and forth.

Even if they didn't believe everything was alright they would make to calm the pack down. It was their job.

Singing Crow glanced around and let out a sigh. "Warm Daisy and her mate will stay with us, they can be much help to us, because I'm assuming she's a police officer?" The female barked, closing her beautiful eyes. "You all are to respect them, even if you don't like them very much." She shot a glare at Scrawny Raven when those words spilled out of her.

Scrawny Raven rolled her eyes, knowing it was targeted at her. "Yeah, what she said." She growled, letting her gaze level to those around her. "Bumble, Racing Creek and Loud Tail will show Warm Daisy and her buddy around, since I'm sure they all need to learn where their loyalties lie." The female barked, her voice now much calmer than before. Her gaze was still cold towards Warm Daisy though.

Racing Creek jumped up with excitement and a howl escaped him. He quickly shrunk down with a chuckle. "Sorry!" He murmured, a smile emerged on his face. More family time for him. His tail was swishing back and forth, almost as fast as the speed of lightning.

Scrawny Raven rolled her eyes and went on to tell everyone their duties for the day. Before, she did all that though she decided to tell all the council members something. Were they talking behind their backs? Were they keeping something from the pack?

Loud Tail rested his tail on the male, a chuckle escaping him. "Y'know, I'm surprised you even caught that rabbit earlier since oh you're so terrible at hunting them. Not enough brains in that small head of yours." He teased, poking Racing Creek with his paw.

Bumble tilted her head, furrowing a brow. "Oh, so another thing to tease my bro about?" She laughed, bouncing up and down. Her tail was swishing back and forth as she circled both of the males. Loud Tail of course was much taller than her, since he was the tallest canine in the pack, but she was taller than Racing Creek.

The female had left her vest somewhere else, most likely in the den she had made for herself but she couldn't remember. Her heart was pounding against her chest. What if someone stole her jam. She could make more but those were the only bottles she had. Plus, Red would never get replaced. He was her booby plush and it would always stay that way, till the day she died.

Huckleberry walked over to them and dipped her head at Bumble. She rolled her eyes at Warm Daisy and giggled shortly after. "My name is Huckleberry and yours?" She questioned, introducing herself to one of her tour guides. She hadn't met this one yet but she had met her wife's son and his friend, Loud Tail.

"The name's Bumble." She greeted, dipping her head before slapping Creek, bowing down. "I'm Racing Creek's sister, he's so lucky to have me!" The female announced, tail swaying back and forth as they started to exit the camp. Her eyes were bright as she leaped up to snatch a flower from the tunnel. It was a rose this time, but with no thorns, someone must have placed it there.

Huckleberry glanced over to Warm Daisy, furrowing her brow. "Oh? Another pup you haven't told me about?" She questioned, sending a glare at her wife who wasn't even paying attention to her. The female was too busy sniffing the ground.

Bumble shook her head softly. "Warm Daisy isn't my ma," The female barked. "My pa is Haboob and my ma is Paige." The female told the Siberian Husky, tilting her head to the side.

She was watching the blood pour down the female's shoulder. Her tail was limp as she tilted her head to the side. "I don't get why they told us to show you around when you're bleeding!" She exclaimed, shaking her head. Her eyes were wide as the female just licked the blood off.

Huckleberry shrugged. "Could be worse, dealt with much worse after all." She barked, following Loud Tail as he sniffed the ground leading them somewhere. Her tail was swaying back and forth as she leaned against the female who continued to sniff the ground. She was tempted to push her but decided not too.

Bumble let a whimper run through her like a rabbit being chased by a deadly fox. Her tail continued to be limp as they neared a large rock which Loud Tail leaped up onto.

"Pack members gather around!" He barked, raising his paw as he summoned them. His eyes were closed as he let his ears listen to the sounds of nature. Birds were chirping singing their daily songs, bringing life to the forest like they always did. A smile emerged on his face as he opened his eyes realizing that his group was gathered around, chuckles escaping all of them.

He opened his maw to speak, his ears twitching. "I have come to say that the new alpha of our pack that will stand beside me will be Racing Creek!" The male announced, licking the cheek of Racing Creek when he leaped onto the rock. Both of their tails were swishing back and forth and Warm Daisy watched with eyes filled with warmth.

Bumble opened her maw and howled. "Racing Creek!" She cheered, tail swishing back and forth, forgetting her recent conversation with Huckleberry. Her ears were perked up and she jumped up. "When we get back to camp after this tour, we can celebrate with some of my world famous jam!"

Loud Tail jumped down with a laugh escaping him. "I'd love that." He barked, rolling his eyes.

The male turned to Huckleberry and Warm Daisy. "So, that's Alpha Rock, it's where most rookies go when they want to fool off." He told them, his voice leveled. "Trainers will bring their rookies there to test their eyesight and their sense of smell." Loud Tail explained, towering over the two.

Bumble tilted her head to the side. "Should we bring them to the sand pit?" She asked, tilting her head to the other side. Her tail was swaying back and forth; she opened her maw again to suggest something else. "We could take them to the abandoned pond!"

Racing Creek glanced up at the sky. Their time was almost coming to an end. It was dangerous strolling around at night now. "We can go to the sand pit, we'll show Huckleberry the pond later, but it's almost night." The male barked, following Loud Tail who led the way to the sand pit. It wasn't too far.

Bumble nodded, a smile painted onto her face as she followed all of them. Her paws were crunching down on stray leaves and sometimes acorns threatened to trip her. The female's ears were waving around from the wind that danced around, having a battle with one and another.

Redwood trees were waving by the slightest, a hallucination made from the wind. Nothing would be strong enough to chop those trees down. Shrubs were climbing up them as they walked, their pace steady as they walked. Wind was tugging at everyone as the day drew to an end.

A large dip in the ground was near, filled with sand. Sometimes they brought pups out to play here, but rarely. The forest was dangerous for young pups to wander. Hawks would fly by and cougars would prowl. Lonely female dogs would try to take them and raise them as their own. So many possibilities.

Huckleberry glanced around, uneasy as the sand tried to get in between her toes. "I like this place?" She barked, tilting her head to the side. The female didn't look too fond of everything at this very moment.

Warm Daisy lowered her body to the ground, wiggling her haunches before launching. She tumbled into the female, growling playfully at each other till one ended up at time.

Huckleberry looked smug over her wife, a smirk crawling onto her face. She bent down and bumped her nose against her nose. Her tail was swishing back and forth as she gazed into the brown eyes of Warm Daisy. "Your eyes are beautiful, they might not be as blue as the ocean but they represent the earth. The earth holds the most beauty anyways. The earth brought us together." She murmured, her voice stunning as she spoke.

"Your eyes are the same color," Warm Daisy chuckled. "Does that mean I can do the same thing?" She asked, rolling her eyes while her pelt heated up.

A smirk danced onto Loud Tail's face and he let out a

gasp. "Look! There's an ant!" He called out, waiting to see Racing Creek's reaction. His tail was swishing back and forth and he cackled as the male jumped up onto his two mothers. Making them all tumble over.

Huckleberry whispered a curse and threw Racing Creek off of her.

Racing Creek scrambled back onto her though. He glanced around searching for the ant that was crawling around. "You won't get me from up here Mr. Ant!" The male yelled down at the sand, not knowing where the ant could be hiding. His tail was tucked between his quivering legs as he continued to whip his gaze around.

CHAPTER NINETEEN

Racing Creek dipped his head and murmured something to Loud Tail who was currently chowing down on a hare. His tail was swishing back and forth as he nuzzled the male Golden Retriever before he turned away. The male was going to try to hunt as much as he could so everyone could have a feast.

He was put on duty this time along with his sister, Ancient Willow. Each time a pup was turned into a rookie the newest members of the pack have to hunt so they can have a feast in celebration. Of course, they would extra help with hunting but they would be the main dogs that would be hunting for this celebration they were going to have.

"Wish me luck!" Racing Creek barked, a smile wide on his face. His eyes were bright as he passed the den; he listened to some of the gossip the dogs were saying too. Nothing too juicy to spill though. His tail was continuing to swish back and forth as he exited the tunnel. Fragile lower petals falling down on his back.

His spine shivered as a breeze slid down it like a pup on a sunny evening. The male shook his head firmly, admiring the beauty of the trees that were littering the forest. They were tall, reaching the sky with their claw like branches.

Squirrels were fighting over nuts, playing tug n war. Even though they were an easy target right at this moment he didn't go for it. He would need to scout out the area to see what kind of prey were scavenging. He might be able to find a baby deer too, but that would all depend on luck.

Shrubs were pressing up against his legs like kits would crawl up to their mothers when they were ready to feast. The sun was shining down on him, gifting him light to help him find prey to bring back. The sun god was on his side today, what a surprise. Usually the sun god would burn him from something he did. Maybe the sun god was only doing this because this was for the two pups in the nursery.

Birds were chirping, singing their songs. Racing Creek never got sick of them, all of them were beautiful in their own ways. But, squirrels were a different story, their little annoying squeaks bothered him so much and oh my dog when they throw stuff at him is the worst. Could they just stop? The answer to that question was a no, they would never stop. Racing Creek did something to them yet he didn't know, he would never know.

His paws steps were silent as he took in the scents of the forest. He could hear the faint yells of the pups in the camp, celebrating the fact that they were going to become rookies. As a pup that's all you would think about, restless, but when one is a rookie they regret it all, wanting to go back to their puppyhood.

When was he going to hunt? Well, that's a perfect question, Racing Creek himself doesn't even know the answer to that.He was going to hunt when he felt like it. When the time felt right. Which would probably be soon, but the time didn't feel right for him at the moment.

The scents of hares, mice, and much more mammals ran through his nose, teasing him. He let out a sigh, opening his maw. "I guess I could start now." He murmured to himself his voice almost inaudible. It wouldn't do any harm and there's a bunch of prey here! The male swibled his ears to the side, listening carefully to the pawsteps of the prey that walked. If he could get in tune with at least one of them he could find out where they were going and make up a short but quick plan to capture it.

He lowered his belly to the ground, putting his ebony colored nose on the ground. He would go after the hare. It could be plump and he wouldn't want to ruin his chance. He would also try to find some voles due to them being the pups favorite prey. He had to hunt as much prey as possible to make everyone happy and fill their bellies.

Soon, the hare came into view. It was much larger then any rabbit he'd seen, well they were supposed to be bigger then rabbits so it made sense. He stalked forward, silently, trying to look for any escape routes it might have. He couldn't lose this one. He just couldn't. He wouldn't mind losing a different catch but this one was really plumo. He would gain the packs trust back even more. Not that he lost his packs, trust it as just that they were all cautious because of the scroll and with his mother back with a stranger dog. It was all chaotic times.

The hare's nose was twitching when it nibbled on grass, not knowing what it's destiny was going to turn out to be. Its haunches were scrunched up, ready to make a run for it if it needed too.

The male stalked forward, rolling his shoulders. His paws were light on the ground, he couldn't let it hear him. Wiggling his haunches, he launched himself at it, surprisingly the hare was too plump to be able to have the right reaction at the right time. It was too slow. His teeth were fixed into its throat and he shook his head aggressively, making sure it was dead.

He dropped the hare. "Are you dead?" Racing Creek questioned, tilting his head. He didn't receive anything so a smile emerged on his face. His tail was swishing back and forth as he grabbed with his maw. He just needed to find a hole to put it in now.

The male glanced around, searching for a good area to hide his prey. He could probably do it beneath one of the trees, where there was a hollow trunk. It wouldn't be a bad idea but he would need to hide it really good, so no fox would be able to come and take it. Racing Creek glanced around before trotting to somewhere else, in search of an area.

Crunching leaves when he approached, he dropped the rabbits. The male entered the hollow tree trunk and started digging, continuing to glance behind his back to make sure that there was nothing trying to snatch it from him. This was his prey and no one else's.

When he made the hole deep enough, he turned around and sunk his teeth into the scruff of the rabbit. The male dropped it in the hole and jumped up, not being able to hit his head on the roof. "That's one and many more to go." He sighed, exiting the tree.

Racing Creek lifted his nose, letting the scents drift into his nose. His tail was swaying back and forth as the scent of a mouse nest danced around his nose as it was teasing him. He lowered his belly to the ground, his heart pounding against his chest. The male's ears were pressed up against his head as he glanced around, cautious of his surroundings.

The mouse nest was near this den, there was no way they didn't hear him. They were most likely huddling up with one another afraid of the aggressive canine that was to come. Racing Creek would dig up the area, and plunge his snout in it, forcing them to try to make a great escape. It was one plan he could do. It wasn't the best plan in all the world but it was a plan.

The male circled the tree, his brown eyes narrowed. His tail was raised, unable to sweep up leaves to disturb the mice even more than he already was. Next, he made his paws much lighter, hopefully this would calm his prey down.

He stopped at the side of the tree where the scent was stronger than the other places. The male bent his head down, peering into the hole that was placed into the tree. His tail was raised, wiggling his haunches. He could make out little brown shapes that were all huddled together. Squeaks escaping the terrified mammals.

The male started to dig, dirt flying up into the air. His claws were clawing into the soil, attempting to squeeze his snout in. This really wasn't the most effective way to do things but here he was. Doing it. After a while of digging without stopping, he managed to squeeze his whole snout into the ground.

The mice squealed, trying to scramble away. Luckily, he could fit his paw in too. He managed to hook one of the mice on his nails. Tail swaying back and forth as he drew the mouse closer and at the perfect time he snapped its neck.

Racing Creek should be able to get at least one more mouse. It shouldn't be that hard too. They were all running around, shock and grief running through their tiny bodies.

He swiped his paw at one of them, catching it off its guard. The male hooked his bloody nails onto the creature and dragged it towards him, repeating the process that just happened, snapping its neck swiftly.

The male backed up, a sigh escaping him. He dragged the mice out with him and sunk his dagger sharp fangs into their scruffs. Racing Creek would simply bring it to the hole and drop it in there, well he would need to dig it back up again. As a hunter, he loved hunting so of course he would end up hunting again for the celebration, but with his sister that'd be a different story, she was a guard.

He bounded over to where the entrance of the tree was and started digging the hole back up. Once, he was done he dropped the prey down into the hole before piling the dirt back into it. He bent his head over and he grabbed a hold of some grass and put it on the lump of dirt. "Perfect," Racing Creek whispered. His tail was swishing back and forth as he shook his pelt.

The male bounced out of the tree, in search for more prey. Racing Creek could go to the pond to fish, the pack hasn't had fish for a while. A lot of the pack members did like fish but the pups haven't tried it before so this was this perfect time to get some.

His paws were pounding against the ground acorns threatening to make him trip and fall. Leaves were continuing to crunch under his boulder-sized paws, ears flattened against his delicate skull. He glanced around, his eyes drizzling over the tall thick trees. The trees he glimpsed over at had moss climbing them, flowers blooming, like dandelions and daisies.

The male let a sigh escape him as he slowed down his pace, admiring the beauty that had passed him. His tail was swaying back and forth as he neared the pond. It had a dock that was covered with moss, threatening to fall off the deep end. It was beautiful. Frogs and toads would hang out there, holding meetings in the circle of mushrooms. Lizards would often cling onto the bottom of the dock, watching for straying flies.

"There better be some fish here." He mumbled, climbing onto the dock. His legs were wobbling, afraid of the whole thing tumbling apart, like the dogs in his pack. The male looked down at the water, a reflection of something in the water.

There were three dogs, all Golden Retrievers. The tallest one had creamy white fur while the other one had slightly darker fur and then... there was him. He slammed his paw into the pond, making the image break instantly, nothing left of the faces that haunted him.

Shaking his head, he decided to watch for the shadows of the fish that would pass. This would be a waiting game but it was going to be worth it in the end. He would have a bunch of food to bring back to the pack. They would all be so proud of him.

A shadow started to swim toward him and he let his paw hover over the pond. His haunches were wiggling and his heart pounded against his chest. He would catch this, he knew he would. Well, hopefully he would catch it.

Racing Creek sent his paw down into the water, his nails scraping at the fish but unable to catch it. "Moose scraps!" He cursed under his breath, his ears swiveling to the side.

The dock was creaking. Someone else was on here with him, but who? He turned his head slowly to be eye and eye with a coyote. They were wearing a blank bandana with bones crossing each other. Was this one of the coyotes that the scroll-maker was talking about? Scars were littering the canine's pelt, other than that it looked really clean. She had brown fur with black streaks going through it.

"Ah, your one of the weaker canines, she was talking about." The coyote cackled, her paws were coming closer and closer to Racing Creek. Her tail was swaying back and forth as she caressed his cheek with her paw. Her ears were pressed up against her skull as her snout twisted, showing off her sparkling teeth.

The male backed up, paws threatening to slip into the mossy pond. His ears pressing up against his skull as he stared into the eyes of the coyote. Racing Creek's tail started to quiver as the female continued to walk towards him, her pose deadly.

"Scared?" She barked, tilting her head to the side. A smirk was fixed onto her face as she gazed at him, satisfaction dancing in her chestnut colored eyes. Her tail was slowly raised, cackling as she continued to near Racing Creek. When she got no answer, she rolled her eyes. "Well you should be."

Racing Creek stepped forward, gathering the courage. His tail was still quivering as each second went by but it was still raised. The male's nails were digging into the ground as he studied her. One of her toes were twisted, but that couldn't possibly be a weakness, could it be though? "Nice, toe you got there."

She closed her eyes before letting them snap open. The female licked her chops as she stared at him. "Checking me out now, aren't ya?" She barked, laughter escaping her as her whole facial expression disappeared, blank. Her silence was becoming eerie, quick. The female lowered her stance, wiggling her haunches. She leaped forward, paws stretched out.

Both of them tumbled into the water, pelt soaked. Paws were being slammed against the water, trying to keep their heads up.

"Why did you do that?" He yelled, his gaze hardening as he attempted to swim over to her. The male's paws kept making droplets fly into the air as he continued to try to swim over to the female but she kept swimming away. His ears were flattened against his skull as he shook his pelt while he was still in the water.

The female rolled her eyes, yet another laugh escaped her. "Well, you see I'm not allowed to kill you." She explained, sticking out her bubblegum pink tongue at the male. "So, like if I *accidentally* pushed you into the pond and you drowned it wouldn't be my fault." She was so bluntly honest, it amazed Racing Creek.

"You're going to get it!" Racing Creek growled, swiping at her cheek with his nails from afar. His eyes were hardened as he tried to swim away, not wanting the coyote to actually try to drown him. His tail was tucked beneath his shivering legs as he swam away. Fishes were scattering around, not wanting to be involved in this mess while toads were croaking, cheering for one of them.

The female scoffed and swiftly swam to where he was swimming. He was going to get it. No one messed with her and got away with it. She set both of her paws on the male's head and shoved him down. The female unlike the rest of her group would show mercy, she just wanted to let the canine know that she should be feared, it was as simple as that.

Bubbles were brought up to the surface, struggling to breathe. His head bobbed up, gasping for air, but then he was shoved back down. Racing Creek's paws were frantic, kicking every possible thing that got in his way. He wasn't here for her drowning him.

She let go, for good this time. "Don't slap me again!" The female snarled, her fangs sharper then thorns and daggers combined. "I will drown you for real next time if you do." She growled, rolling her eyes at the male who stared at her like she had just ate a toad.

"You're breath stinks." He barked, shaking his head, droplets once again flying everywhere. "Smells like a stinky toad, a really stinky one." Racing Creek told the female, no mercy shown in his voice as she stared at him like a rabbit on a sunny day. His tail was starting to be lifted by the water itself, as he calmed down.

A growl was rippling in her throats but she swallowed it. "Let me bring you to the shore and dry you off." She stated calmly, sinking her teeth into his scruff. The male was heavy but not too heavy to the point where he'd drag both of them down into the pond. Her paws were making fast and strong movements, bringing them to land much quicker then Racing Creek would be able to swim to land.

"Uh, thank you?" He barked, getting water in his mouth when he spoke. The male ended up coughing until they were both on land. His tail was swaying back and forth as he shook his pelt, droplets spraying onto the Coyote who did not look impressed at all.

She opened her eyes, her fang poking out on one side of her snout. "Yeah, no problem." The female growled, rolling her eyes. "Thank you for spraying me with a bunch of water." She barked, with a fake warm smile approaching her face as she gazed at him.

The male shook his body once again, his tail swishing back and forth as he watched the coyote dry off. "No, problem!" He barked, a frown shown on his face. "Why are you being nice though? Aren't you one of those coyotes involved with this whole murder mess in my pack." The male explained, eyeing her suspiciously.

"I am involved with their group but I don't support what they're doing." The female barked, dipping her head. "The forest is huge, miles and miles, so I don't get why they think that they should have the whole forest to themselves." She explained, her pointed ears pressing up against her head. "Anyways, the name is Primrose." She told the male quickly.

He nodded, taking in all that she had to say. "Pretty name, my name is Racing Creek." The male announced, raising his head, proud of the title he had earned. His tail was swaying back and forth as he gazed at her, it was like he knew her before, but he couldn't put his paw on it.

"Yeah, thanks." Primrose murmured, taking off her soaked bandana. She shook her fur once again when he spoke. "I already know that's your name, congrats on the title." The female barked, sliding the bandana over to him. Her tail was swaying back and forth as she gazed at him.

"What's this for?" He asked, his head tilting to the side. His ears were perked as he glanced down at the bandana then back up at Primrose. *Why did she give me this? I mean I know what it is, but why would she give it to me?* The thoughts ran around his head as he stared at the female, confusion dancing around in his dark colored eyes.

"Take it." She ordered, glancing around cautiously. Her tail was starting to tuck beneath her hind legs when she heard the birds chirp their daily songs with beautiful harmony. "I've known you since we were both pups so if I die, I want you to have it." The male barked, her voice soft. "They're always listening, Creek, stay safe." She barked firmly, grabbing the bandana once again and sliding it over onto Racing Creek's neck.

The male watched her, unable to find words.

"Stay safe." She repeated, sliding into the shadows that the forest had gifted them.

This was it. He had carried all the prey that he had caught to the pack. In the end, he managed to catch a hare, two mice, and a vole. It wasn't much but it would have to do. His breath was thrown out of him, trying to catch his breath when Loud Tail approached him. The male's tail was swaying back and forth as he watched the broad-shouldered canine walk over to the prey pile.

"How did you get all wet?" The male questioned, his head tilting to the side. "Also, what's with that bandana?" He asked, his eyes starting to narrow. His ears were pressing up against his head as he watched Racing Creek open his maw, trying to think of something to say. He rolled his eyes, plopping his rump down.

A howl broke out in the camp and dogs gathered around, smiles were shown on their faces. Today was a big day. Everyone enjoyed this day. Especially the dams who took care of these members. The pups loved this ceremony more than anyone else though.

"Today is a special day for all in the Tumbling Stones Pack." Scrawny Raven announced, raising her head as she let her gaze drizzle over the dogs who were crowding around her and her mate, Singing Crow. "Today is the day that two of our pups will become rookies!" She barked, her voice was loud and clear when she spoke.

Singing Crow dipped her head, the opposite of what the other alpha had done. "Those pups are Bear and Pigeon, they both have reached the age, five months. They are ready to become rookies." She announced, a smile emerged on her face. "Both of them will be training along with Birch." The female continued on with her unprepared speech.

Scrawny Raven jumped down from the log she was standing on. "Bear, step forward." She barked, watching the young canine shrink down and crawled over. His eyes were watery as she gazed up at her and a whine was rippling through his throat.

"I...I don't want to become a rookie without my brother by my side." Bear whined, the sun avoiding his pelt, leaving only darkness for him. His whole body was shaking as tears ran down his cheeks. "Can... he... can he become a rookie with me even though he's dancing in the stars?" The pup questioned, shrinking down once again. His tail was tucked in between his legs as whimpers and whines continued to escape him.

Singing Crow nodded at what he had to say, jumping down to stand beside the female. She licked the tears off of the young pup. "Of course, when the time is right he'll earn his full name too." Her voice was soft, like she was always meant to be around pups.

"Oh ok!" He barked, his tail swaying back and forth as he gazed up at the two alphas. "I'm ready to become a rookie!" Bear told them, fluffing out his chest as he spoke. Any dog could tell that he was doing this for his brother who had sadly passed away. "I'll do this for chase!"

Scrawny Raven lifted her snout in a howl, setting her paw on the small canine. "May our ancestors accept you as one of us!" She howled, her eyes closed as her voice danced around the air. The female brought her snout down and licked the side of Bear's cheek. "You are now a rookie, may you try your best to protect and hunt for this pack."

The same thing repeated but for Pigeon the slightly older one, she wanted to wait till the brothers could become rookies with her.

CHAPTER TWENTY

Bumble walked up to Racing Creek, her head tilting to the side. "What's with the bandana?" She questioned, her voice sweeter than her jam could ever be. Her tail was swaying back and forth as she stared at him, not getting an answer. "I promise I won't freak out if it's really unbelievable." She chuckled, jam sticking to her paws. The small whickers that littered her snout twitched as the male started to answer.

"I got it from an old friend, her name is uhm..." He could feel eyes shooting into his back. "Her name was hibiscus." He mumbled, glancing away from Bumble. The male gazed down at the black bandana he wore, it complimented his fur color well, but did it really suit him?

Bumble nodded, turning her head away with a small smile approaching her face. "That's nice of her." She murmured, continuing to look around for Muddy Ears. She might have been on rookie duty though, so that would mean they couldn't spend the day together again like they usually do.

A large male approached the two dogs, a nervous smile glued to his face. "So, uhm... uh... Bumble.. Can I talk to you?" He asked, his head tilting to the side. His tail was swaying back and forth slowly as he gazed at her, but it quickly moved down to his paws like a rockfall. Rippling River's floppy ears were starting to press up against his head when he didn't get an answer. "Please?"

Bumble plopped her rump down, her tail swaying back and forth. "Sure," She barked. The female furrowed her brows. Her head tilted to the side as she waited for the male to tell her what he wanted. She wasn't that impressed with him at this very moment.

"Alone?" The male asked, lowering his head. His tail was slowing down when she glanced over at Racing Creek. He shrunk down, paws shuffling against the grass. Rippling River's eyes were travelling over to the exit of the camp. He could go grab a flower to convince the canine to go out and talk to him. The male ran over to the exit, jumping up to pull a daisy out from the tunnel. Rippling River ran back over to them and placed a daisy at Bumble's paws.

Racing Creek raised a brow as he stared at the large male. He really was trying to impress Bumble. This didn't go well for him and a growl rippled through his throat. He wouldn't do anything but if anything was to happen to Bumble, blood would be thrown around.

"Fine, I'll go with you." Bumble barked, rolling her eyes. She jumped to her paws, glancing back at Racing Creek. "Why don't you go hang out with your boyfriend?" She teased with a wink. Giggles were escaping her when she saw that Racing Creek was heating up at what she had said.

"He's not my boyfriend." The male mumbled, glancing away. "Go hang out with your popular friend now." Racing Creek barked, refusing to meet her eyes. His tail was curled around his body as his gaze swirled over to the bandana he was wearing.

Bumble rolled her eyes with a small chuckle rippling through her. "Yeah, right." She turned around and started to follow the male out of the camp. The female wanted to see if he had something important to say to her and give her reasons why he was ignoring her for the past days. It better be a good reason.

"So, I uh set up a place by the pond, I worked hard, and have been planning this for a couple days now." He told Bumble, lowering his head. The male didn't want to seem tall at this moment because right now he was the opposite. He was a whole mess. His tail was swaying back and forth though, he didn't want to seem too friendly but he wanted to seem friendly. He didn't know what he wanted! The male's paws were thudding against the ground as he walked beside the female.

Bumble nodded, taking in what he had to say. "So, this is

why you have been ignoring me?" She questioned, her head tilting to the side as her eyes grew restless. Her tail was not swaying back and forth instead staying till, dangling from her. The jam bottles on her were clapping against each other, threatening to crack.

"I... no." He answered, shaking his head softly. "Scrawny Raven and Singing Crow had us doing some stuff for the past few days." The male explained to the female, a small smile approached his face. He sighed, glancing around at the trees that were towering over him. Shrubs were scattered around, brushing up against his thick-furred legs.

Bumble nodded, letting out a grumble under her breath. "Mhm." She mumbled, raising her head up. Her ears were perked as she listened to the songs that the birds had sung along with the squirrels bickering with each other, arguing about what flavor of acorn was better. The ripple of the pond that they were nearing made the smallest sound as they neared it.

"Sorry." He mumbled, his voice sincere when he spoke. The male crawled onto the dock that was covered in moss, flowers blooming in the oddest places. His tail was swaying back and forth as he plopped his rump down, letting a thud bounce off the trees. The male's eyes were soft as he gazed at the beautiful lily pads that were sitting in the pond. "Y'know they're almost as pretty as you." He chuckled, gifting Bumble with a toothy grin, he looked idiotic but sweet.

She rolled her eyes and looked down at her paws. The female didnt want to look at him, not after what he did, but if she could just steal a small glance from him. "Thank you." She murmured, letting her gaze drift off to the lily pads that Rippling River was staring at.

"I was just telling the truth, Buzz." He purred, now gazing at the female, admiration swirling around in his eyes, like stars on the night sky. His tail was now thudding against the dock, furs falling through the small cracks that the dock had held. Before getting a reply he jumped to his paws and ran off.

"What's he doing now?" She questioned, mumbling

under her breath. The female watched him fade into the shadows but within seconds he came back with a crown of some sort. A flower crown? No. It couldn't be a flower crown. He was holding a toadstool mushroom it looked like. Maybe he made a toadstool mushroom crown just for Bumble.

The male trotted back over to where she sat looking down at the water. He dropped the crown he had made at the female's paws. His eyes were wide as he looked for validation out of Bumble. Rippling River's tail was swishing back and forth as he watched the female put on the mushroom crown.

The mushroom crown that he made was made out of toadstool mushrooms with daisies mixed in with it. Vines were weaved between them, keeping them in place. Moss was hugging them, not letting them out of their grip, they wanted to make sure the crown was safe away from the dangers that hid in shadows.

"It's beautiful," She murmured. Her eyes were stunning as she gazed at the male, her teeth poking out. The female gazed down at the rippling pond, admiring the beauty of the crown that the male had made her. Her tail was swaying back and forth as she jumped to her paws. Her head was tilted to the side as she stared into the eyes of Rippling River who stood there. "Now, really why did you bring me here?"

He looked down at the water that reflected off of the both of them. His tail was swaying back and forth as he admired the beauty of the canine that stood before him. "I... I wanted to ask you if you would be my mate... till we grow old...?" Rippling River asked, lowering his head. He wouldn't make eye contact just in case if she rejected him. His eyes were starting to water when he didn't get an answer but he clawed them down, making sure they stayed down too.

Bumble jumped to her paws and shoved her snout in his thick fur, nuzzling him. "Of course, I'll be your mate." She purred, breathing in his scent. Her ears were pressed up against her skull as she snuggled closer into his pelt. Her tail was swaying back and forth as he placed a paw on her back.

A warm smile approached his face and danced on it, like this was above the happiness he had ever felt in his life before. His tail was thudding against the ground as he let the warmth from the female crawl onto him. The male's heart was pounding against his chest as he gazed down at the female. "I have something else planned out too." He murmured, hugging her tighter.

She backed out of the hug, blinking. "Well, what's that?" The female questioned, her head tilting to the side. Her eyes were focused on the male who stood there, glancing at her vest. She had two full jars of jam while one of them was empty from the pups sneaking in and eating it all.

"I was wondering if you wanted to make some jam with me?" The male barked, forcing his gaze to travel down to his paws. His tail was still thudding against the ground as he stared down at his paws. "I already have the ingredients you told me about ready!" He barked, now staring at the female with wide sparkling eyes.

A giggle escaped Bumble as she gazed at him. "I'd love to do that." She barked, glancing around. "Now where are the ingredients that you have ready?" The female questioned, her head tilting to the side. Her tail was swaying back and forth as she stepped paw on land and not on the mossy dock.

"They're actually in a tree." He told the female, running off into the shadows, wanting her to follow. His tail was raised and slamming against the angered wind.

Bumble sighed and leaped, getting a headstart with chasing him. Her paws were pounding against the soggy ground that soon turned sturdy. Roots of trees were everywhere and acorns threatened to trip her. Her tail was swishing back and forth as she glanced around at the beauty as she ran. The birds were singing songs like they were made just for her and only her.

They soon reached a large tree with some sort of house built with it. There was a staircase swirling around the redwood tree and leading to the house. Vines were hanging off with flowers blooming and moss tried to take over the stairs. Birds were sitting on the branches, singing songs, while the squirrels once again argued about what flavor of acorn was better. There was always some sort of fight going on with the squirrels.

"What's this?" Bumble asked, her head tilting to the side as she gazed up at it. Her eyes were climbing up the stairs and reaching the house within a matter of seconds. The female's tail did not stop swaying back and forth but she couldn't help but let curiosity dance around her body.

Rippling River started to walk up the stairs, glancing back at his mate. "Well, it's a treehouse. It was built before the pack was made so rookies usually sneak up here to get away from angry parents." He explained, raising a paw before setting it back down not wanting to fall off. "It's safe I promise." The male barked, watching Bumble cautiously place a paw onto the stairs.

"It better be safe." Bumble murmured, her eyes focused on where her paws were. She couldn't help but glance around though. It was a beautiful sight, no one could deny that. Vines were threatening to fall onto her back and tickle her. Her tail was sticking out like a branch, keeping balance.

He rolled his eyes as he glanced back at her. "It is safe." The male barked as he climbed into the house. His paws made a thud against the floorboards as he walked in, it bounced around the house and onto the trees. Chewed up chairs were placed while rope toys were thrown around. There was indeed a kitchen though, moss filled but it worked. There was an oven and a freezebox there.

She followed him and glanced around the house, all seemed familiar but that was only because she grew up in a village. There was a bowl of berries along with a small bottle of honey and sugar. "Oh, so you really did get all the materials I usually use." Bumble chuckled, padding over to where the kitchen was. A wide smile was shown on her face. Her tail was also swaying back and forth as she grabbed the empty jar out of her vest.

Rippling River raised his snout with a chuckle. "I wouldn't lie, would I?"

A cackle came from the stairs and there stood two coyotes ready to attack them. The scroll-maker really wasn't joking around when she said she'd make sure that no one would be left if they didn't start to leave. "Y'know, I really thought you poor little puppies would decide to leave this forest. After all it is our territory now." Barked a coyote who held a fake pouting face. His fangs were poking out while his tongue threatened to escape him.

The female beside him pushed him with a snarl. "Put your tongue in, dumbo." She was wearing the bandana Racing Creek had. Both of them were wearing the same bandana. Was Racing Creek involved with all of this? Her sparkling fangs were bared as she glared at everyone in the house.

CHAPTER TWENTY-ONE

The male looked down at the note he was writing. He was in the middle of the forest inside a tree trunk. Racing Creek couldn't let anyone know what he was doing. *Is this alright? Will they take this as a war cry?* The thoughts raced around his head as his heart pounded against his chest.

He opened his maw to read it out loud to make sure it sounded well. His tail was curled tightly around his body as he whipped his head around, refusing to read it out loud. *It would be better if I read it in my head.* The scroll he used to write on was torn and drenched in water but he was still able to write on it with berry juice and his nail although he did manage to get squirts of berries all over it.

DEAR, ANONYMOUS
RACING CREEK

Hello, coyote gang. My pack and I will not move out of this forest, this is our home. If you want it you'll have to fight us for it. We won't give our home up for you skinny rascals. The forest can be home to both of us, but if y'all want to take it all, you'll have to fight for it. We won't give up. The forest might end up being a bloodbath but Tumbling Stones Pack will always win against you mongrels. We will always win. You may go after us at our weakest times but we won't give up. We won't give up.

Love, Racing Creek.

The male nodded at what he had written on the scroll.

His tail was swaying back and forth as he curled the scroll back up in a tight ball. Now, it was time to bring it to the place that the scroll-maker had told him to bring it. This may start a war but it was worth it.

Those canines had to learn that they weren't going to let them push them around any longer. They had killed two of their pack members and they couldn't let more get killed. They were on the last straw. If no one was going to write back to them, Racing Creek did the right thing.

He bent down and gripped the scroll in his maw. His tail was swaying back and forth as he glanced back and forth. A sigh escaped him as he exited the tree trunk, feeling the breeze dance through his long fur. His ears were pressed up against his skull as he started to walk away.

Leaves were crunching under his paws as he moved away, his nose twitching as scents raced around the air. Acorns were also being thrown away carelessly, some hitting Racing Creek in the back causing his head to whip around and threaten the squirrels with his dagger sharp teeth.

The trees were passing his gaze each time he lifted a paw up. Dogs would pass him, not suspicious of him due to him being a hunter. Everyone had their duties to fulfill in this pack. He didn't have any patrols he had to go on today so maybe he could hang out with the Puli pups.

There was a pair of eyes that were digging into his back, he could feel it perfectly, to perfectly. The dog was near or coyote? He couldn't tell anymore, it could possibly even be a hyena at this point. The male didn't turn around though, he had a mission and he was going to complete that mission.

He shook his head as the scent of a coyote ran around his nose. He wouldn't just stop because some coyote was near. The male glanced down at the bandana and squeezed his eyes shut. Primrose was so paranoid the day she gave him this. Something could have happened to her but he swallowed the fear down.

The male's paws were making a pounding sound against the ground as he fastened his pace. His ears were slowly perking up as he reached his destination.

Mice were squirming around, nibbling on berries they had found. This was the time they were able to scavenge for food due to the owl being asleep. This was the safest time for them. Safe time is the best time for them. Their little tails were the last to be seen as they all snuck into a hole at the sight of Racing Creek.

The male walked in front of the tree, glancing up at where a hole was drilled into it, owl snoozing. He lowered his head and dropped the scroll. He did it.

He needed to get out as quick as possible though, he couldn't risk being caught. His tail was swaying back and forth as he whipped around. A smile was emerging onto his face as his paws crunched above the leaves that strayed and his paw pads rolling over acorns.

"Why did you do that?" A voice questioned, her brows furrowing. It was Primrose. Her tail was raised as she glared at him. Her eyes were narrowed into slits like she disapproved of what he had just done. The female's pointed ears now held notches in them along with a silver arrow piercing through one.

Racing Creek tilted his head to the side. "Do what?" He asked, his voice innocent, possibly more innocent then a pup's voice. His tail was swaying back and forth as he gazed at the female, but he glanced down at the bandana that was wrapped around his chest with a sigh.

She shook her head softly. "Play dumb, Creek." The female murmured, sadness clinging to her voice. "Just remember when the forest is a bloodbath, it all leads back to you." Primrose barked, raising her snout as she walked away. She was so mysterious yet Racing Creek felt like he needed to be by her side. She was like a better sister. There was a reason why he didn't talk to Ancient Willow anymore and that story wasn't to be told.

The male let out a small snort but decided to leave like she did. He wasn't going to go after her just because she walked off after being so vague with her words. His paw steps were now being dragged against the ground like he was forcing them to leave.

I wonder what was up with her. Plus, why would I start a bloodbath in the forest. No dog in their right mind would do that. The thought ran around his mind as he continued walking back to the camp. He couldn't help but wonder what Rippling River wanted to talk to Bumble about since he did want to talk alone. Did he apologize for ignoring Bumble or was he just asking to go hunting? May the world never know.

His tail was swaying back and forth as he glanced around at the passing trees. Camp wasn't too far at least he thought. It was like a five minute walk, so yeah it wasn't far at all. Acorns continued to be scattered around along with flowers that were pulled by the wind.

A scent danced around his nostrils and he looked up to see a tall male in front of him. It was Loud Tail with a worried expression on his face. "Where were you?" He questioned, licking the side of Racing Creek's face. His tongue had darkened to a more dull pink, it could have been how the sun was reflecting off of it though. His tail was swaying back and forth as he walked to the entrance of the camp, glancing over his shoulder.

"I was just walking around the territory, why?" He questioned, his head tilting to the side. Loud Tail never acted this worried, well at least with him. They were getting closer by the day though and some dared to tease them about being a couple.

Loud Tail opened his maw to say something but Poisoned Rowan walked forward with her snake wrapped around her neck. "Rippling River and Bumble got attacked by a couple coyotes." She explained, glancing over to the worried Loud Tail. "You're little boyfriend over here is worried that you got hurt." The female barked, taking in the scent of Racing Creek. "Afterall, you do have the coyote scent written all over you." Poisoned Rowan whispered, not wanting to alarm the others in the pack. "I won't question you this time but next time be prepared for the council members to take you in for interviewing."

"Oh, oh..." His voice trailed off as he brought his gaze

back to his paws. "So, uhm if you don't mind I'm going to go and see Squawking Parrot's pups..." Racing Creek barked, bouncing away, not wanting to get involved with the mess involving what he smelled like. His paw steps made the smallest thud against the ground as he neared the nursery.

He poked his head in with a smile painted all over his face. The male was looking at the female Puli who wrapped herself around her pups. "They look beautiful." He commented, letting his eyes glaze over the small dogs who fought each other to get to their mother's belly. Squeaks were heard as one and another pushed one aside wanting to get all of the milk for themselves.

"Thank you." The dam murmured, watching her three puppies strive. Her tail was swaying back and forth softly while Flowering Tulips was in a deep slumber.

Racing Creek tilted his head to the side as he watched the female's young pups. "Have they opened their eyes yet?" The male asked, bowing his head as one squeaked. His tail was swaying back and forth as he watched them turn their heads to look at him but they quickly went back to their milk.

She nodded, her black pelt shaded by the shadows that swarmed around the nursery. The puli looked down at her offspring with warm in her eyes, possibly warmer than a fire at a campsite. Her tail was swaying back and forth as she watched them with an eyesight better than a hawk would ever be able to have. "They still refuse to talk though but when they do I'm sure they'll be talking non-stop." She chuckled, watching them wiggle.

"I can't wait till that." Sarcasm was coating his voice. The pups once they started talking were like parrots, repeating everything everyone said. They also went after his tail, his tail was prey for them, they could've gone for anything but they decided to go for his tail.

Huckleberry approached him from behind and yanked his tail. "You told us that you would show us the pond someday and someday is today." She barked, scoffing. The female still wore her vest but she had a new scar from when she fought with the canine who gave her the scroll she brought back. "Also, I'm the only one you have to show since Daisy is out hunting."

The made nodded, taking in what the female was saying. He dipped his head to the dam and turned to his step-mother. "Yeah, I'll show you it." He grumbled, walking towards the exit, glancing around at the dens that were scattered among the camp.

"How far away is it?" The female questioned, itching her ear with her hind paw. Her ears were pressed up against her skull as she glanced around. This wasn't her home but she would try to make it her home. If Warm Daisy was going to stay, she was going to stay, they didn't marry each other just to leave each other.

He shook his head softly at the question. "You'll see how far away it is when we get there." The male growled, looking back at his tail which had just been yanked. His ears were pressed up against his head as he sent a glare towards Huckleberry. The male's snout was lifting in a snarl but he quickly watered himself down.

Huckleberry lifted her brow as she gazed at him. "What's got you in such a knot?" She questioned, her head tilting to the side. The female's tail was flicking side to side, still having patches of fur missing on it. Huckleberry's ears were starting to bounce back up as he spoke.

"You." He answered, plopping him rump down to lick his tail. His eyes were focused on his tail but they travelled to Huckleberry to see her reaction to what he had just said.

The female nodded and turned around. "Remember where you stand pup." She snarled, thorn sharp teeth shoved into Racing Creek's face. Her tail was raised and her ears went back to being pressed up against her fragile skull. The female's paws were shuffling in the grass as Racing Creek did the same.

"I stand higher in this pack then you stand." He growled, a chuckle rippling through him. His tail was swaying back and forth as he stared into the eyes of his mother's wife. Racing

Creek couldn't help but look down at her vest which was on her tightly. "Why are you still wearing that? Scared? Proves that you'll always be a scrawny Village Dog."

"I don't think village dogs are scrawny, we actually have food unlike you stinky mongrels." She growled, glancing down at his bandana. "Check what you're wearing before trying to diss your other mother for what she's wearing." The female barked, rolling her eyes.

CHAPTER TWENTY-TWO

Poisoned Rowan plopped her rump down in the den, playing with the seashells she had stolen from the alpha's den. The snake that she had was wrapping around her paw this time, climbing up her leg. "Can you tell us about what happened?" She asked, her head tilting to the side by the slightest. Her tail was swaying back and forth as she sat.

Singing Crow nodded at what the council member had said. She sat next to her mate, Scrawny Raven, listening to what the couple had to say. Her tail was curled around her broad body as she watched everyone carefully as they all shuffled their paws against the dirt.

"Well, so you know that treehouse everyone goes too?" Rippling River barked as he sat next to the female. His eyes were focused on the alphas as they let their gaze drizzle over him and the other dogs. The male's tail was swaying back and forth as his floppy ears were pressing up against his skull.

Scrawny Raven nodded at what he said and opened her maw to respond. "Mhm." She mumbled, slouching down. Her tail was swaying back and forth as her ears swiveled to the side, listening to what was happening outside of the den.

"Well, Bumble and I were there making jam and uhm well I guess they followed us up there." Rippling River told them with his head lowered. Bumble was leaning against him as he spoke. Tail swaying back and forth as he watched his pack member's reactions.

Gray Wind shook her head roughly. "You didn't smell

141

them?" She barked, raising her snout. Her eyes were focused on Rippling River and Bumble like a hawk.

Bumble lowered her gaze down to the ground. "Yeah, we didn't." Her voice trailed off as she felt Gray Wind's harsh glare dig into her spine. Her ears were slowly pressing up against her skull as she lifted her gaze to look at Gray Wind who just sharpened her gaze.

"Then why do you two have noses if you're not going to use them?" Gray Wind questioned, furrowing her brow as she glared at them. Her curled tail was limp, twitching only a little bit. Her ears were pinned back against her skull as she waited for them to respond.

Scrawny Raven rolled her eyes at what Gray Wind had said. "You know for a matter of fact that almost every canine in this world knows how to hide their scent." She growled, her eyes narrowed as she watched the council member. Her docked tail was twitching as the female didn't respond to what she had said. "Oh, so you're not responding because you know i'm right or are you just at a loss of words because I'm right?" She asked, her head tilting to the side.

Gray Wind let out a small inaudible grumble, glancing away from her alpha. Her eyes were focused on her paws, not daring to let them reach Scrawny Raven's eyes. She scoffed and rolled her eyes as the twins started to giggle under their breaths.

Singing Crow raised her paw and sent a glare towards the two Saluki's. "Were they wearing anything? Did they have any scars?" She questioned, her head tilting to the side. Her tail was swaying back and forth as she watched Bumble start to open her maw.

The black bandana with the crossed bones. She couldn't tell them that, they'd suspect Racing Creek to be on their side. Bumble did remember the female coyote had a slash on her cheek and nose though, wherever she got those scars from must've hurt. "Well, uhm, the female had a scar on her cheek and nose." The female told the alphas. Her tail was swaying back and forth as she anxiously gazed at Rippling River as if to tell him don't share any more information.

Rippling River nodded at what she had said. "The male couldn't control his slobber." He added on, with a chuckle running out of him like a frightened mouse. His tail was swaying back and forth as he watched the council members whisper things to each other.

Bumble glanced around, her nose raised. The coyote scent was everywhere and it burned her nose. Why couldn't they all get along. She gripped the plush tighter, not wanting to let go of her childhood. Her tail was swaying back and forth as she watched Muddy Ears run ahead of her. "Wait up!" She called out, her paws pounding down against the ground.

Muddy Ears rolled her eyes as she glanced back at the female. "Yeah, yeah. I'll stop for you, girly." She barked, her ears twitching as she gazed at the female. Her tail was swaying back and forth as she gazed at the female, waiting for her to catch up to her.

Bumble took her sweet old time as she walked up to Muddy Ears. She glanced around once again, paranoid that there might be a coyote at every corner. "I wish we all got along with each other." She mumbled, looking the female in her sweet brown eyes. The female was gripping the plush even tighter this time, anyone could be surprised that she hasn't ripped it in half yet.

"What do you mean?" Muddy Ears questioned, her dark brown ears flopping to the side. Her eyes were travelling around the place, climbing each tree.

Bumble shook her head softly and laid down, rolling onto her back. "You know dogs in this pack and the coyotes." She groaned, looking up at the female who stood over her. Her tail was flopped over laying on the cold ground next to her. "It's tiring. Why can't we all become one big family?" The female asked, her ears flopping onto her side.

"It's just not going to happen." Muddy Ears murmured, laying beside the female. Her tongue was lolling and drool fell onto the ground with a small splatter of droplets. The hunter's tail was swaying back and forth as she laid her head on Bumble's paws.

She shook her head softly. "Why not?" Bumble questioned, her head tilting to the side.

"It's... just impossible for us to get along I guess.." Muddy Ears mumbled.

CHAPTER TWENTY-THREE

"Primrose!" He called out, desperate. The male needed to see the coyote, this was one of his last hopes. She had stormed off last time but if they were going to war... because of *him*. His tail was tucked between his quivering legs as his ears pressed his skull. The male stepped forward once again, his gaze continuing to glance around but they eventually climbed the trees, in fear that coyotes were able to climb them.

He plopped his rump down letting a sigh run out of him. "Primrose!" Racing Creek called out again, his paws stretching out. His tail laid limp as his eyes darted around. Would he be allowed to take her into the pack? He already brought two dogs into the pack. Primrose wasn't a dog though... She was a coyote. His pack and coyotes aren't getting along either right now. Maybe if he brought Primrose though, he could change things a little bit, maybe they'd trust Primrose once they got to know her.

A pup crawled out of a bush, twigs and leaves stuck in her fur. "Why are you calling for my ma?" She questioned, a whine rippling in her throat. Her tail was tucked beneath her shivering hind legs and her pointed ears were pinned against her skull. She wore a necklace that had a skull hanging from it, an owl skull by the looks of it.

"Well, uhm I'm friends with your mother." Racing Creek explained, frozen in shock. Why hadn't Primrose told him that she had a daughter. Did she have more pups without him knowing? His tail was as still as a branch on a humid day. He opened his maw to speak again but nothing else came out. "I... I... uh well uhm I need her for something very important."

"What if you're lying to me and you don't need her for something important?" The pup growled, her eyes narrowed as she watched the taller dog. The hybrid glanced around before raising her snout in a howl. "Ma, Pa!" She howled, whines rippling and mixing in with it. The female howled once again, much louder and urgent this time though.

A fluffy male came running and Racing Creek recognized him. It was Kit. His ears were pressed back and his snout was twisted, showing off his sharp fangs. "Racing Creek?" He barked, his eyes going wide with fear as he backed up. "Please, don't tell the others about this..." The male barked, his voice frantic.

The pup looked at him and tilted her head. Her ears bounced up and she hid under his belly. "What do you mean by that?" She questioned, her eyes wide as she looked up at her father. Her tail was swaying back and forth as she saw Primrose walking over to where they were. "Hi, ma! This strange dog wanted you, he even smells strange." The female barked, scrunching up her nose in disgust.

Primrose shook her head with a sigh. "Be nice, Rose." She murmured, dipping her head in greetings to the Golden Retriever. "What do you want?" The female asked, her head tilting to the side. Her ears were swiveled to the side.

He bent his head down, ignoring the curious gazes of Kit and Primrose. "I... well Primrose can you come to the pack? We might be able to convince them that not all coyotes are bad!" He barked, tail starting to sway back and forth. "What do you guys think about that?" The male asked, his head tilting to the side as he brought his gaze up to gaze at them. His tail slowed down when he didn't receive a response.

The pup looked up at her father with her maw parted in awe. "Oh my coyote, can we go! Please! Please! Please!" She whined, her honey-colored eyes watering. "I've always wanted to see your pack! You're always there, never spending time with me!" The female barked, running in circles as she waited for her parent's response. A smile emerged on her face as she looked up.

Kit shared a small glance over to his mate. "I guess, but don't be sad if they don't allow us to stay." He murmured, his tail flicking side to side as he spoke. His gaze was focused on the young female who continued to look up at him, begging.

Racing Creek backed up, shrinking to the ground as he watched the family decide. His tail was swaying back and forth as he tilted his head to the side. This reminded him that he needed to talk to his family more, maybe after all this he could go talk to Warm Daisy and Ancient Willow. They could all do things like they used to do.

Primrose pushed Racing Creek to the side. "I see, you're still wearing my bandana." She chuckled, glancing over to Kit. "Hey, since Creek over here has brought like a million dogs in the pack you should bring Rose in, honey."

Kit nodded and started leading his daughter to the camp. Shrubs were brushing up against his thick-furred legs. His paws made a pounding sound against the soft earth. His ears were pressed up against his skull while his tail was swaying back and forth. "See you soon!" He looked behind his shoulder to call over to Primrose.

"If the forest does turn into a bloodbath don't expect me and my daughter to stay." She growled, her eyes cold as she gazed at Racing Creek. The female had clearly read what he had written in the scroll. Her tail was raised and her ears were flattening against her skull.

He shook his head softly. "Primrose, nothing bad is going to happen!" The male growled, his fur standing on edge. "You're so worried about this whole scroll I did that you never bothered telling me that you had a pup with one of my pack members." Racing Creek barked, his voice bouncing off the trees.

"Well, I'm sorry you never asked!" She shot back, pushing him to the side as she made her way to the camp. The fur that lined the female's spine and tail was raised. Her eyes didn't turn back to see Racing Creek's reaction, she simply didn't care what happened. "Take care of your bandana, I hope no one figures out where it comes from." She commented with a small giggle escaping her.

"I will let you stay for now but if you cause any drama or lay a paw on any of our pack members, I will not show mercy." Singing Crow announced, her gaze drizzling over her pack members who didn't seem to like her idea. "That my dear is a promise."

Scrawny Raven stood on the log beside the alpha. "There's also a rule that everyone must go out with at least one dog by their side. All is getting too risky. Coyote scents have increased."

Cinnamon shot a glare towards Kit. "So we're just gonna let him get away with having a disgusting pup with a coyote!?" She growled, her rump on the damp grass as anger swirled around her eyes. Her tail was raised along with her fur.

"The discussion is closed." Scrawny Raven growled, sending a small glare towards the female. Her tail was twitching as she stood tall, gazing down at her pack. "We'll need some patrols, I'll let Rippling River plan them out though, so all of you are to listen to him." The female barked, raising her paw.

Racing Creek bounced over to where Rippling River was standing. His tail was swaying back and forth and his ears were pressing up against his skull. "Can I take Ancient Willow and Warm Daisy on a border patrol?" He asked, with a head tilt.

The male nodded with a small grumble escaping him. "Of course." He murmured, lifting his gaze. "Be back for the full moon feast though." Rippling River ordered, his voice firm when he spoke to the younger canine. His tail was swaying back and forth as he watched Racing Creek run off to greet his family.

The male's tail swishing back and forth as he ran over to his family. He leaped onto his sister, paws stretched out as he licked her face. His ears were pressed back against his skull when his sister pushed him off with a growl rippling through her throat. "Get off of me!" The female drew her lips back in a snarl. The fur that lined her back was raised as she glared at her brother, her nose scrunched up in disgust.

He stepped back, clearly taken back at her reaction. His ears were pressed up against his skull as he stared into the cautious eyes of Ancient Willow. A whine was rippling through his throat as he stared at her. "What...?" He mumbled, watching her movements as she turned away from him.

She shook her head softly, tears forming in her eyes. "Don't act so innocent!" The female growled, her tail raised as she glared at the male. Her ears were pinned back against her skull as she watched him.

Huckleberry and Warm Daisy got in between the fighting siblings. Growls were tossed around along with insults. Tails were whipping back and forth as glares dug into each other's backs.

Time had passed and the siblings were pulled apart. Everytime they were together one of them would reject the other and nails would be on each other's faces. It was pure havoc.

Prey was being piled up in the middle of the camp. The full moon would be up shortly with the stars dancing around it, worshipping Moondancer, the dog who sat on the moon. Moondancer was a beautiful black Labrador Retriever, known as the Moon Goddess. Every month when the full moon approaches them they would all set up the full moon feast in honor of Moondancer.

Squawking Parrot's pups were complaining that they wouldn't be able to try any of the prey. All of them went by the names of Soot, Hibiscus, and Fawn. One male and two females. Soot was the only one who looked like his mother while the others were a brownish red color. They would be able to join in the feast next full moon though.

The next full moon would be in winter. It always snowed a lot so they had to trek through the snow to find their prey. A lot of the time it would go above the heads of the smaller dogs in the pack, making it extremely hard for them to carry out their duties to serve the pack. He had hope that it wouldn't get this bad though in the upcoming winter.

A howl broke out into the camp as the darkness started to dance around everyone. Stars were going to come out to play shortly. "Today is the full moon, meaning that we will have a feast to honor Moondancer in giving us darkness to sleep in peace." Singing Crow announced, her tail swaying back and forth while her eyes drizzled over everyone.

Rose swished her tail back and forth, a smile emerging on her face. Racing Creek could make out the words that she was saying to her mother, Primrose. "Pa, always told me about Moondancer and how she was his favorite goddess! I want to be like her someday, sitting on the moon!"

A smile was painted across his face and a chuckle escaped him, not loud enough to cause a disturbance among the pack though. His tail was swaying back and forth as he watched the dogs run in circles in excitement while others let out cries.

"Pups will eat first along with storytellers then the dams and so on." Scrawny Raven barked, her docked tail not making any movement, it was more still than a rock that was too stubborn to be moved.

Racing Creek watched Rose walk curiously over it but a younger dog had snapped at her. Her father was going to come and defend his daughter but the two dams were already at it saying Rose had a right to get something to eat because she was a pup, even if she was part coyote.

His tail was swaying back and forth and he walked over to where Primrose stood waiting for everyone to grab their share. She would eat scraps if it came to her not being able to grab anything. "She'll be safe here." He murmured, his voice a bit muffled from grabbing a bird from the pile.

Believe it or not, birds were one of his favorite prey but it was often rare for anyone to actually catch one so he took it. Feathers would often end up choking him when he was trying to eat the bird, but the bird was delicious so he'd take the risks.

"Hopefully, she will be," The female growled. She could sense the aggression coming from some of Racing Creek's pack members and if she had too again she would show aggression right back at them. When everyone left the prey pile, she left Racing Creek to grab her own prey. "I'm disappointed in you, *Racing Creek* I really am." She mumbled.

CHAPTER TWENTY-FOUR

Bumble looked at Primrose before looking away. "So, uhm, how's it going?" She asked, trying to start a conversation. Her tail was swaying back and forth as she licked at the jam she had placed on the leaf. The female had Red, her booby bird plush, right beside her.

"Fine," Primrose responded dryly. Her tail was raised along with her nose. "Aren't we supposed to be hunting, not clinging to a stuffed animal and eating jam-?" She questioned, a chuckle running out of her. Her tail was swaying back and forth by the tiniest bit.

"We're *supposed* too." Bumble barked, a small laugh escaping her. "I don't mind bending some rules sometimes if it means that I get to eat some jam!" She barked, shaking her head due to getting some jam stuck on her cheeks and nose. Her tail was swishing back and forth as her ears flopped over, continuing to shake her whole head.

Primrose slid her nail onto the female's ebony colored nose, getting rid of most the jam that sat on her nose. She licked it off her nail and her face scrunched up in surprise at the taste. "Y'know I always doubted this jam but once you actually try it, it's pretty good." She complimented the female, glancing at her cheeks and yet another laugh tried to burst out of her.

"Oh my dog, can you stop looking at my cheeks like that?" Bumble questioned, rolling her eyes. "Also, thank you!" She barked, dipping her head and gripping onto her plush. "Should we go over to the pond and see if we can catch any toads or lizards?" Bumble asked, her head tilting to the side as she questioned the female.

"Sure!" Primrose responded, hopping to her paws. Her tail was swaying back and forth as she took the lead, making Bumble question something.

She tilted her head to the side, her ears flopping to the other side once again. "How do you know where the pond is?" The female asked, suspicion growing and dancing in her stunning eyes. Her tail didn't stop swishing back and forth it only continued, even though what happened was strange she wasn't going to let it ruin her happiness.

"Well, I've lived around here for a while, I know a lot of dogs in your pack even if they act like they don't know me." She explained, raising a paw as she spoke. "There's some canines you don't know about that live around here, we got grandma Peach that I don't think any dog in your pack knows about." Primrose murmured with a sigh. "Before you ask who Grandma Peach is I'll just tell you, she's like a mother to all coyotes except shes way older, she makes peach tea for her visitors and she's the sweetest coyote you'll ever meet in your lifetime."

"Can I meet her someday?" The female asked, her head tilting to the side. A smile was spread out on her face like jam on toast as she gazed at the coyote. Her tail was swishing back and forth even faster, maybe grandma peach and bumble could collaborate someday and make limited edition peach tea jam. It would be a dream.

Primrose raised her snout and let out a sigh. "I guess we could go right now, we'd just have to be quick since your pack is expecting us to hunt." She murmured, glancing around, keeping track of her mental compass that she had.

"Oh my dog! Really?" Bumble started to spin around in a circle as she was overjoyed in the news that she had just received. Her tail was swishing back and forth as she watched the female turn away from the direction of the pond and deeper into the forest, ignoring the towering trees. The female bounded after her, her tongue sliding out of her mouth.

Primrose nodded, chuckling at the female's reaction. She looked back at the female and furrowed her brow at Bumble's belly but said nothing. Her tail was swaying back and forth as she looked ahead. "Why do you want to meet Grandma Peach so badly?" The coyote asked, a questioning tone rolling off her tongue, yet it was soft and not demanding like most would have when they wanted an answer.

"Well, you see I always wanted to make tea and we could make peach tea jam together." Bumble explained, raising up a paw as she spoke. A smile was painted on her face once again yet much bigger than before. Her ears were pressed up against her head as she watched a flock of birds fly south. Her tail was continuing to sway back and forth but faster then it has ever gotten. This would be one of the best things to happen to her in her whole life!

"Oh, is that so?" Primrose barked, furrowing her brow. Her ears were bouncing up and down as she walked, leaves crunching under her paws. She shook her head softly after a while though. "I can already smell the winter coming." She mumbled, her voice sank. No one liked winter well at least in the packs, it meant less prey and more sickness, luckily they had neighboring villages that would give them medicine though. They wouldn't want to take the medicine that they were given but it would help them survive.

Bumble dipped her head with a small sigh. "Yeah, winter is coming, I'll be stuck with the pack for the whole winter." She mumbled, sadness edging her voice, she wasn't planning on staying this long but plans changed and dogs died. "No more travelling." The female barked, her voice quiet though, not as loud and clear as before.

"Oh? So, you like to travel the world for a living?" She asked, tilting her head to the side. "If I'm being honest, I think you'll stay in the pack since your mate is living in it." The female commented, raising her paw into the air as she spoke. Her tail was swishing back and forth as she noticed Bumble's surprised reaction at what she had said.

"Where did you find that out?" She asked, raising a brow. Her ears were flopping all over the place as a bounce was placed in each step of hers. The female didn't mind that Primrose knew, she just wanted to know how since she knew Rippling River didn't tell anyone and she hadn't either. If one of them did tell others in the pack they would tell each other. They would.

The female opened her maw to speak. "Well, word spreads around fast." She murmured, lifting her nose to take in the scents of the tea that swarmed around, pulling in visitors. Her tail was swaying back and forth as she watched the shrubs dance as wind ran around them like small pups chasing after one and another.

"Yeah, I guess." She murmured, her tail starting to swish back much faster as the tea scent reached her nose. Her head tilted to one side as her maw parted in a long yawn. "Are we almost there?" She questioned, excitement circling her voice. Her ears were bouncing up and down along with her paw steps as she fastened her pace.

The female nodded, a smile emerging onto her face as a small cottage with vines hanging off, flowers blooming from it.

An eldery Coyote sat on the porch, sipping a cup of peach tea. The female's tail was swaying back and forth as her large snail sat beside her. Humming escaped her as she noticed the two canines. "Come in! Come in! We can all share a lovely peach tea." She barked, her eyes bright as she fixed them onto Primrose and Bumble who were starting to make their way over to her.

"We're coming, Grandma Peach!" Primrose barked, fastening her pace, wind tugging at her short fur. Her ears were perked as she watched the old coyote dip her head in a welcome. The female's tail was swishing back and forth, watching the snail make a trail as it followed its owner into the cottage.

Grandma Peach led both of the canines into her cottage, her tail swaying back and forth. She wore a peach orange bonnet that had a lime green trimming. The humming continued as she made her way into the kitchen, heading over to where she had kept the tea she had just boiled up. Peaches were piled up on the countertops along with tea bags. "Welcome to my cottage!"

Primrose nodded, a toothy grin spreading onto her face. "I've been here before but thank you very much." She murmured, her head lowered to the ground as she made her way into the living room. Her tail was swaying back and forth as she jumped onto one of the fruit shaped pillows, Grandma Peach had. She was sitting on the purple grape plush.

Grandma Peach tilted her head to the side with a chuckle escaping her. "Well, your little friend hasn't." She murmured, dipping her head to Bumble. "Go ahead, take a seat one one of my cushions." The female barked, her voice soft.

"The peach one is my favorite and the better one." Grandma Peach murmured softly, a few moments later. She made it so the coyote couldn't hear her, she obviously picked favorites once in a while. Her tail was swaying back and forth as she watched Bumble jump onto the peach plush that Grandma Peach had just told her about.

Bumble dipped her head at the words of the wise eldery coyote. "Thank you," She murmured. Her tail was swaying back and forth against the wooden floor. The female's paws were shuffled, making the tiniest scraping sounds against the floor with her nails.

"Your welcome, my dear." She murmured, her tail swaying back and forth. "Does everyone here like peach tea?" The female questioned, her head tilting to the side. "I have plenty and I'm willing to share." Grandma Peach announced, her nose raising while the tips of her fur bristled as she waited for an answer. Her gaze was darting from the dog to the coyote.

"I would love to have some tea!" Bumble barked, her rump wiggling as she watched the older canine pour tea into cups for them. Her eyes were focused on the female, leaf green eyes sparkling. She hadn't had tea in a long time, she had it when she was in her home village and that was about two years ago.

Primrose let out a small grumble in response. "Yeah, that would be nice. Anything we can do to pay you back for the tea?" She asked, her voice smoother then the waves that would climb onto the sand where her mother had lived. Her tail was curled around fragile body as she listened to the humming that Grandma Peach was doing, she was humming some kind of song.

"Oh no, dear, you don't need to pay me back with anything." Grandma Peach murmured, bringing the teacups over to the coffee table that she had. Her tail was swaying back and forth as she watched the two females grab the tea that she had made for them. The female after refilling her tea sat on an apple cushion.

The female tilted her head to the side. "Are you sure?" She asked, a smile emerging onto her face.

"I'm sure." The female barked, sipping her tea. Her tail was swaying back and forth while her ears were flicking side to side as she waited for someone to speak.

Moments went by and she set her teacup down. "How is everything going for you guys? Bumble how is your pack doing, I haven't been there for years." She murmured, her eyes scanning the room. The female's rump was wiggling attempting to get comfortable on the apple cushion.

"It's been well," Primrose mumbled, her tail curling around her body. "My daughter, Rose, has been wanting to see you lately but we haven't been able to visit you." She barked, dipping her head softly. The female turned to Bumble, letting her have a turn at answering Grandma Peach's question now.

"I uh don't live in the pack but uhm it's doing great." She lied, a forced smile clinging to her face. Her tail was swishing back and forth as she continued to drink the tea she was gifted. The female looked down at her nails then back over to the coyote's who had hers painted a pastel orange color. "You have very pretty nails." She complimented, taking yet another sip of her tea.

"Thank you, Bumble." Grandma Peach murmured, her tail swaying back and forth. "Would you guys like your nails to look like mine"

"Thanks for having us!" Bumble barked, her tail swishing

back and forth as she exited the cottage. Flowers were dotting her pelt and her nails were painted a pastel yellow. Her tail was swaying back and forth as she watched Primrose have one last conversation with the eldery female. She also wore bee clips in between her ears, they weren't permanent though.

Primrose bounced out of the cottage with a sigh. "That was some good tea back there." She barked, licking her chops as she jumped off of the porch. Her tail was swishing back and forth behind her and instead of having pastel yellow nails like Bumble she had hers painted a pastel blue due to thinking it would match her pelt. She had a necklace with some tiny peach plushies that Grandma Peach had made.

"We have to go hunting now!" Bumble barked, excitement swirling off of her voice. "Let's hope we don't get our nails messy." She chuckled, her ears flopping over as she bounded off into the direction of the pond. Her tail was swishing back and forth right behind her as she watched Primrose pass her.

Primrose let out a bark as she slowed her pace, letting the younger female catch up to her. "Yeah, but prey for your pack is better than our painted nails." She barked, her voice loud and clear as she spoke. Her ears were perked up, alert for any sound that would prowl into hearing range. It was getting late out and it wasn't an option to let prey run by them.

Bumble followed the female, a smile emerged onto her face. "Thank you for letting me meet her by the way!" She purred, lowering her head as she let the scents from the earth gather up and dance around her ebony colored nose.

"No problem." Primrose barked, lowering her body to the ground.

They dropped all the prey they had caught in the prey pile. They managed to catch three toads, four lizards, and a fish. It was quite a lot of prey, not a lot of dogs would be able to catch that in a limited time frame. It now had hit night, stars partying in the sky along with Moondancer who watched over everyone.

CHAPTER
TWENTY-FIVE

"Hey, you two!" An unfamiliar voice barked, the fur on the coyote bristling as he watched the larger dogs. His tail was raised as his gaze grew colder as each second went by. "Do you know Primrose by any chance?" His lips were threatening to draw back in a snarl as he waited for a response.

Loud Tail sharpened his gaze as he looked at the Coyote who was staring directly at him. "I do not know Primrose, sir." He had to keep himself from growling, keeping his voice calm and collected. His tail was slowly raising, the fur on it bristling.

"I sense a lie." The coyote snarled, starting to circle around the two males. His paws were silent as they slammed down against the soft earth while sunlight reflected off of his yellow stained teeth. The male's tail was whipping back and forth as he glared at the two. His ears were also chaining themselves against his head, twitching only the tiniest bit.

Racing Creek rolled his eyes with a scoff. "Yeah, well we aren't lying." He growled, stepping back while his nails dug into the soil beneath him. The fur that was lining his spine and tail were bristling each time the coyote took one step towards them.

"Oh, another lie?" The coyote snarled, tilting his head to one side. His tail was flicking side to side as he glared at the two males. "I won't harm you, if you decide to tell me the truth." The male barked, his voice spiked with daggers.

"We are telling the truth." Loud Tail growled, letting his tail raise much higher than before. "Even if we did know

Primrose why would we let a random stranger know that." He barked, his voice getting much louder, letting the dogs that prowled near know that they could be in trouble. His tail was flicking side to side as he noticed that Racing Creek was starting to edge closer to him.

A growl rippled through his throat and he launched towards the large Sarabi Dog. "Watch your mouth, mongrel." He snarled, locking his maw onto the male's ear, blood started to flood in his mouth as Loud Tail started to shake the male off.

"Get off of me!" Loud Tail shrieked, his voice filling with panic as the male let go. The coyote was holding half of his ear, blood covering his snout. His eyes went wide as the coyote dropped what he was holding only to launch himself at Racing Creek this time.

Racing Creek let out a shriek of pain as the coyote tugged on his tail only to shoot down to his ankles, nipping at them, threatening to hook his fangs onto them. The male quickly managed to kick the coyote in the face, ears pinning back as the male screeched.

"Let's get out of here." Racing Creek growled, starting to run off, his paws pounding against the ground. He glanced over his shoulder to see the coyote cursing under his breath. The male also saw that Loud Tail was running right beside him.

Loud Tail's whole face was bloody from the blood that was pouring down his torn ear.

Time had passed and they both plopped their rumps down in the grass. Both of them were sitting in the camp with dogs starting to circle them, throwing questions at them. The shamans soon took them into their den though, shooing the others away.

Once they made it into the den, Cleared Sky had furrowed her brows. "What happened?" She asked, getting the herbs that they would need ready. Her voice was sweet, sweeter the honey could ever be and that made the bees jealous. She held some cobwebs and she held some chewed up goldenrod on a leaf.

"Well, we were patrolling the border and he jumped out asking if we knew Primrose." Racing Creek explained, raising one of his front paws when he spoke. His tail was swaying back and forth as he watched the female put the herbs onto the male's ear. "We lied to them of course, because we didn't know his intentions and he saw right through them I guess. He attacked us right after, taking Loud Tail's ear with him." He explained, raising his nose into the sky as Jagged Paw checked out his hind legs.

Loud Tail nodded, flinching at the touch of the paste to his ear. His paws were shuffling on the dirt as his tail swayed back and forth. "Yeah, everything he said happened." He mumbled, lowering his gaze down to the dirt as he continued to flinch as Cleared Sky put the paste onto the ground. "The dumb coyote managed to take part of my ear too."

Jagged Paw took one last sniff at Racing Creek's hind ankles. "You should be fine, just take it easy." He mumbled, walking out of the den to get fresh air.

"Okay! So, I can go on a hunting patrol right about now?" Racing Creek asked with a chuckle running out of him. He jumped to his paws, flinching when he put all his weight on his hind legs. His tail was swaying back and forth while his ears were twitching.

"No, you cannot, when I said take it easy I mean stay in camp for tonight and then go back to your duties tomorrow." Jagged Paw growled, his tail flicking side to side. His snout was curled as she pushed the male to the side with a small scoff.

Racing Creek rolled his eyes and his ears flicked to a side as he heard his belly grumble. "Well, if I can't go on a hunting patrol, I'm going to get something to eat since I'm starving." He barked, exiting the den, aiming for the prey pile.

His tail was swishing back and forth as he let the sunlight burn his dark ginger pelt. The male's paws made a small pounding sound as he lowered his maw grabbing a couple of mice and a toad. Teeth hooking into it, not letting go. This was his prey now and he wasn't gonna let some pup jump up and take it from him like the last time.

He plopped his rump down and started to chow down on the prey that he had taken from the pile. The first to go was the four mice he had taken and then lastly the toad. Of course, he was still hungry, he always was hungry but that was enough for now, at least.

"Had enough to eat?" Muddy Ears questioned, her head tilting to the side. Her tail was swaying back and forth but anxiety started to creep into her beautiful brown eyes.

Racing Creek shook his head roughly. "No, I'm still hungry." He mumbled, looking at the scrapped bones he had left on the ground. The meal was good but the toad wasn't his favorite. His tail was swaying back and forth as he eyed the female, curious about why she had come up to him.

"You're always hungry." The female commented, raising her nose. "Have you seen Bumble by any chance?" She questioned, looking away from the male's burning gaze.

The male tilted his head to the side and his ears flopped over. "Why?"

"Oh..." Her voice trailed off as she tried to think of a reason. "Well, uhm, Rippling River was looking for her." She mumbled, glancing around, until she saw Rippling River organizing patrols. His tail was swishing back and forth and for a moment he locked eyes with the Pitbull.

CHAPTER TWENTY-SIX

Bumble looked down at her swollen belly with a sigh. "I guess I'll have to stay in this pack for even longer." She mumbled, bringing her gaze up into the sky. Her tail was curled around herself as she watched the stars dance around. The emale's ears were pressed up against her skull, watching a rabbit run by while the cold breeze swirled around her.

Her paws were shuffling on the dew-filled grass. The female's ears were pressed up against her skull as she continued to watch the stars that danced around the sky. Someone for sure would come and stumble upon her, questioning her on why she was out on herself.

The grass was swaying back and forth as in to tell someone hello and then goodbye. Clouds were hiding, fearful of the powerful Moondancer who sat on the moon. The moon was in the shape of a cat claw, threatening to scratch anyone who came near.

Chipmunks would make small snores as they slept in the trunks of trees while owls flew around, looking for their next meal. Mice were hiding in their dens, but some dared to stray out but those ones were soon to be dead, getting swooped up owls by seconds.

Her tail continued to sway back and forth as she watched the night birds fly through the sky, like they owned every bit of it. They sang their stunning songs, not showing a care in the world to those who were trying to sleep.

"What to do..." She mumbled, shaking her head. "What to

do?" The female repeated, her paw thudding against the ground. Her maw parted in a long yawn as she started to curl up in a ball. Her tail was swaying back and forth.

She woke up to half of her body being hidden by thick brown fur. Snores were heard and she turned her head around to see her mate, Rippling River, sleeping right beside her with his ears pressed up against his skull. His tail was swaying back and forth as his snores continued to get louder.

The morning sky was a masterpiece, the most beautiful painting that Bumble has ever seen. It was full of pinks, yellows, purples, oranges, and blues! It reflected off of their pelts too making them glow in a way they never did before.

She attempted to scoot away, not wanting to wake the council member. When she did attempt to get up and leave though, Rippling River woke up.

His head was tilted to the side and his maw parted in a loud yawn. "Why were you out here all night?" He questioned, tilting his head to the other side as he asked. His tail was swaying back and forth as he watched the *heavy* female start to walk away.

"I just wanted to stay out and watch the stars." She whispered, glancing around, a sigh escaping her. "Thank you for joining me?" Bumble barked, raising her nose into the air. Her tail was swaying back and forth as she glanced behind her shoulder to see the male getting up.

"You're welcome," He chuckled. The male walked over to where Bumble was and tilted his head to one side. "Would you want to go hunting with me? Nothing is better then some early morning hunting." The male barked, shaking his pelt as he followed the female.

"Sure." She barked, stretching her spine. "Where will we be hunting?" Bumble asked, yawning. Her tail was swaying back and forth as she listened to the songs that the birds created for all of them to listen too. It was like they were performing a concert. These ones of course were the birds that didn't go south for winter, these ones didn't want to leave the forest they have always known.

"Your choice, m'lady." Rippling River murmured, glancing around as he waited for a response. His tail continued to swish back and forth as he watched the clouds start to cover the bright sun that was peeking out at them, watching their every move.

She glanced around, her floppy ears perked. "We can hunt anywhere really, I guess." Bumble mumbled, a branch breaking under the weight of her paw. Her tail was swaying back and forth as she noticed Rippling River go down into a hunting crouch. He must have seen some sort of animal run by and knowing him he wouldn't give up free food.

The male ran off into the shadows of the forest and when he came back he was holding a plump chipmunk. His tail was swishing back and forth when he dropped the mammal at Bumble's paws. "We already got one down!" He chuckled, a smile forming on his face. "We'll have a whole pile of food for the pack in no time!"

"Yeah, we will!" She responded, a giggle rippling in her throat. The female pushed her nose down to the ground, hopeful to find any scents that would track to nearby prey. The only scent she could smell at the moment was the dead chipmunk smell that was swirling around in the air right about now.

The newfoundland started digging a hole near the tree they had slept near, dropping the chipmunk in. They couldn't have some stray coyotes or dogs taking their prey that they had caught for their pack. His tail was swaying back and forth as he covered the hole back up in dirt, hiding it from views and hopefully hiding the scent. "Catch the smell of anything, yet?"

"No," She responded. Her head was still held low while

her nose was focused on the scents that were on the ground, even the smallest of scents could lead to a wonderful catch. The female's tail was sticking out like a broken branch as she stalked forward.

Rippling River dipped his head at what he had heard. "We'll just have to go farther out then. Maybe to the owl tree?" He barked, tilting his head to the side.

"Yeah, let's go there." Bumble murmured, fixing her posture and lifting her nose. Her tail started to sway back and forth as she followed the male. The female's ears were perked up, her gaze darting around, carefully watching to see if prey would poke out from where they were hiding.

Rippling River let out a snort as dirt fell onto his back and nose. He looked up to see one of the rookies sitting on a sturdy branch. The closer he looked at the canine though, he realized it wasn't a rookie. Well, a rookie in his pack. It was a young coyote who probably meant no harm to them.

"Sorry!" The coyote pup whined, jumping down, landing in front of the dogs. His ears were pinned back against his skull while his tail swayed back and forth. "Is there anything I can do to make up for it? I know I'm not supposed to talk to you dogs but I feel bad!" The male whimpered, pacing back and forth. "I can try to help you guys hunt!"

Rippling River nodded slowly, watching the coyote's every move. "Okay, you can help us hunt but you have to tell us your name." He growled, his fur bristling. The male's eyes were burning into the young canine's pelt, he wasn't going to trust some coyote at these times. Sure he trusted Primrose but she proved herself to be trustworthy.

"My name is Coyote!" He squeaked, his tail swishing back and forth as he gained more confidence with being around these dogs. His ears were now perked while a smile climbed up and onto his face. "Can I help you guys hunt now?"

Before, Rippling River could respond to Coyote, Bumble barked something. "Of course you can. Don't mind this big guy being grumpy, he's just paranoid." She whispered the last parts to the young canine with a chuckle rippling through her throat.

Coyote ran in a quick circle, his sandy yellow pelt glowing as sunlight bounced off of it. "Let's go!" He howled, jumping forward and showing off his best hunting pose he could do. The male wiggled his haunches and pounced on a leaf. "Look, I caught something!"

"Good job!" Bumble purred, her tail swaying back and forth as she watched the young male. "Rippling River aren't you proud of our new *friend* for catching something?" She questioned, furrowing her brow. The female turned back to the young coyote, a grin shown on her face. "That's a wonderful catch."

"Thank you, miss!" He barked, growling at his tail. His eyes were darting around and a squirrel caught his eye. He immediately went down into a hunting crouch and flicked his tail. The male would catch this squirrel. He had to catch it. He had to make up for throwing dirt on one of the pack dogs. He could get scolded by his parents and he didn't want that.

Moments passed and the coyote had disappeared into the long grass that filled some parts of the forest. He later came back with blood splattered over his snout and a squirrel dangling from his maw. "I'm not the best hunter so sorry it's really messy..."

A coyote entered from the darkness, snout twisted in a snarl. "Why is a young coyote like you, hunting for these mutts?" The coyote didn't even know the young pup but it was one of their species.

CHAPTER TWENTY-SEVEN

He glanced around, a sigh escaping him. The male really didn't know what to do. He was stuck in camp for being aggressive to outsiders. They looked like coyotes! He couldn't just let them pass through the territory without an explanation. It was the only right thing to do! What was he supposed to do, give them tea and tell them to have a nice day?

His paws were shuffling, dirt attaching itself to his paw pads. Nails were digging into the dirt as he glanced around. There was no prey in the middle of the camp so he wouldn't eat his boredom away. Maybe he could go talk to the storytellers and ask them to tell him a story.

He shouldn't though, talking to storytellers and asking them to tell stories was a puppish thing to do. He was a hunter now, not a pup nor a rookie. Asking the storytellers for a story was too tempting to not do though.

The male jumped to his paws and glanced around. Hopefully no one would catch him doing this, well the pups could because that would be no big deal but if the other hunters and guards caught him, his life would be over. Teasing would be increased everyday.

He crawled into the storyteller's den to see Chased Turkeys eying him. "What do you want, youngling?" He grumbled, placing his snout on his large paws. His tail was swaying back and forth as he waited for an answer. Chased Turkeys is basically a grumpier version of Cinnamon.

"Oh... I was wondering if you could tell me a story!"

Racing Creek barked, his tail swishing back and forth as he watched the two share a small glance. His ears were perked up as he plopped his rump down. "I can get your ticks out while you tell me a story if you want..." He mumbled.

"Ok, that's a good deal we can't turn down." Cinnamon mumbled, her voice muffled as she chewed on a bone. Her tail was swaying back and forth as she watched Racing Creek walk over to the much larger dog first.

Chased Turkeys glanced over to where Cinnamon was laying. "So, what story should we tell him?" He asked, his voice holding grumpiness with such delicate care. His tail was swaying back and forth as Racing Creek attempted to get out a tick that was attached to his shoulder.

"Maybe the story about Moth?" The Australian Shepherd suggested, her tongue sliding out of her mouth while drool slammed down onto the ground. Her tail was swaying back and forth while her ears were perked up. She had only heard the story of Moth once with all the time she has been in this pack. She was intrigued to hear it again.

"Maybe..." Chased Turkeys mumbled, letting out a yelp of pain when Racing Creek ripped out the tick he was struggling with. "I'll tell him that one I guess." He mumbled, waving his tail back and forth. "So, it all started when the pack began, there were two alphas." The male murmured, sighing.

"One was the dog we know of as Fading Clouds and then there's Moth." Chased Turkey mumbled, his voice growing softer and filling with sadness. "We're a fairly new pack too, our pack formed about thirty years ago so this wasn't that long ago." He began, preparing to tell the full story.

"Moth was a greedy *coyote*." He explained, shoving Racing Creek into a sitting position. "She brought a gang of coyotes to try to sabotage the pack they had formed. He shook his head softly as he started the next part. "It was like this but the whole forest was covered in blood and it was all because one dog decided to call war on them."

Cinnamon listened carefully, taking in the information

that Chased Turkey's was feeding to them. Her tail stopped swaying back and forth as a picture of what happened entered her mind. It sounded horrible that some dogs had to live through that.

"A lot of dogs here don't tell this story, due to it scaring most of us especially in these times." He murmured, closing his eyes. "We all thought we were at peace with the coyotes but here we are again, they killed two of our pack members."

"Oh..." Racing Creek mumbled, watching the large male tear up as he spoke. He had never seen this male cry, it was just him bossing pups around. He laid his tail on the male who was telling the story while a small whimper rippled in his throat.

"No need to whine, pup." He growled, shaking his head once again. His nails were digging into the soil beneath him. The males ears were pressed up against his head as he stood up, stretching his spine. "Run off now, that's all I will share for a story today."

The male crawled out of the den, wind dancing around and tugging at his long ginger fur. His tail was swaying back and forth as he spotted Squawking Parrot's pups tugging at each other's fur. Their tails were swishing back and forth faster than lightning, they soon hopped over to the coyote pup, tugging at Rose's tail until she let out a yelp.

The prey pile was now filled so he hopped over to where it was and hooked his fangs into a fish. He hadn't eaten fish in a while so it might be good to eat it again. The male remembered it wasn't his favorite last time he ate it but it's a new day!

He padded over to a shaded area and plopped his rump down. The male started chowing down on the fish, careful not to get a bone stuck in his teeth. His tail was swaying back and forth as he licked his chops looking down at the bones and head of the fish.

The male let out a loud burp and chuckled as he noticed the pups staring up at him. "Was it good?" All three of the puli pups asked in unison.

CHAPTER TWENTY-EIGHT

Her paws pounded down against the grass, her nose raised into the sky. She was going to go to Grandma Peach's house again. Shrubs were rubbing up against her legs as she walked, glancing around to devour the beauty that nature gifted them. Her tail was swaying back and forth as the smell of dried tree bark reached her nose.

Not a lot of dogs liked the smell of tree bark but it was one of Bumble's favorite smells along with dew filled grass. It was just refreshing to her, like everything was going to be okay. Another thing that she loved and found fascinating is spider webs with the droplets being caught by them and the shimmering of the moonlight when it bounced off of it.

She would be at Grandma Peach's cottage real soon. Last time she never got to ask for her frog's name and her giant snail's name. They were both adorable. When she got there too, she could ask if they could make peach tea flavored jam! It would be delicious, she couldn't imagine what it would taste like, well she could, she knew it was going to be the best thing ever.

How would she ask the female though? She would have to get reasons on why they should make the jam. What if Grandma Peach wouldn't make jam with her. Her pelt started to heat up and her pace started to slow. She'd have to make up reasons on why they should make jam together.

She was near the cottage and she could see the skinny coyote through the trees pulling weeds out of her garden along with pulling her vegetables. She had to get ready for winter. The female lifted her nose, clearly catching the scent of Bumble.

"No need to hide, dear!" Grandma Peach called out, her voice soft and reassuring. Her tail was swaying back and forth as her eyes drizzled over the trees. The female's ears were perked up as she carefully watched Bumble exit the shadows from where she was sitting.

"Uhm... hey... I have a question." Bumble murmured, looking down at her paws. Her tail was swaying back and forth while the wind made her spine rattle.

"Yes?" Grandma Peach questioned, her head tilting to the side. Her tail swaying back and forth as she waited for Bumble to respond to her question.

Bumble walked over to the female's porch and plopped her rump down. "Would you like to make peach tea jam with me? We could make two batches! One for you and one for me!" She barked, her nails digging into the wood beneath her. A smile was crawling onto her face as she waited for a response, hopefulness dancing on her face.

Grandma Peach nodded, a giggle running out of her. "Of course, let's head inside now, dear." She purred, her tail swaying back and forth. The female opened the door for the *pregnant* female to walk in. Her nose was raised as the scents of her cottage drowned her.

A sigh escaped Bumble as she walked in. Her head was raised, devouring the scents that reached her nose. Her tail was swaying back and forth while her muscles relaxed. The croaks of Grandma Peach's frogs
relaxed her somehow, it was just so relaxing. "Oh, by the way what are the names of your frogs and snail?" She asked, her head tilting to the side.

"Those little rascals? Well, their names are in order, Jelly, Tad, and Rocket." She told Bumble the names of her frogs first and then her snail. They were all wonderful but Bumble didn't get why she named the snail Rocket if snails were so slow.

"Believe it or not, I have never made jam, Mrs. Bumble. So you'll have to teach me." She murmured, waving her tail back and forth as she gazed at the much younger female. Her eyes were a mixture of amber and chestnut brown, but more amber than anything. Grandma Peach's ears were raised as she waited for Bumble's response.

She let a smile reach her face. "Well, we'll need peaches, sugar, and honey!" The female barked, sitting on one the fruit shaped cushions while the elder grabbed the materials they would need. Her tail was swishing back and forth right behind her. Ears pressed back as she looked for the leaves she used for tea.

"I got everything we need!" The elder called, setting everything down on the counter waiting for Bumble to come over and confirm everything.

Bumble got up to her paws and wobbled over to the kitchen. Her ears were perked as her gaze drizzled over the ingredients that the female had put onto the counter. The female's tail was swaying back and forth as she grabbed one of the peaches. "Mind if I try one?" She asked, her head tilting to the side.

"I don't mind at all dear." She murmured, her voice loud and clear. The frogs continued to croak as they hopped around the cottage.

Time had passed and they managed to make the jam. Peach Tea jam they had called it. It would be limited edition due to them not making it again, they had promised to each other that they wouldn't make it without the other canine.

Both of their tails were swaying back and forth while Bumble gripped onto her jam. She hadn't brought her vest with her today to the cottage. She didn't think she would need it even though she was going to ask Grandma Peach about making jam.

Her paws were pounding against the soil as rain poured down slamming into her back. Her ears were pressed back against her skull. This would be a painful way home since this was one of the things she despised. As each second went by, the rain began to get harder and the jam bottle was starting to get slippery. She'd make it home though. She'd make it home to Racing Creek, Muddy Ears, and Rippling River.

CHAPTER TWENTY-NINE

"Why don't you just turn yourself in!?" Racing Creek growled, circling the female who stood there, without a single care in the world. His tail was raised while his fur bristled in anger. "Are you afraid of us? Is that why you killed a *pup* and a *storyteller*?" He snarled, his fangs shimmering as sunlight bounced off of them when he spoke.

The female didn't answer, she only remained silent. The silent that was deadly and eerie. She could jump out on him at any moment. Her tail was raised and the fur on her spine was bristing. Her muscles were relaxed though but they could become tense any moment. She wasn't some dog to be messed with.

"Answer me!" He growled. His tail was kinking back and forth as he glared at the female. His ears were pressed up against his head as he slapped the female in the face, blood falling onto his nails. The male continued to circle the female waiting for an answer he wouldn't receive.

Her paws dug into the dirt and her eyes flashed a honey brown. The female didn't say anything though, only let out an inaudible eerie humming sound. Her tail was flicking side to side as she stared into the eyes of Racing Creek before fading.

The male's eyes shot open and his heart was pounding against his chest. His fur was bristling as he glanced around, his eyes wide with terror. "What... what just happened?" He mumbled to himself, his breathing heavy. The male jumped at the sudden touch on his back but he relaxed when he saw that it was only Loud Tail.

"Hey, relax. It was only a nightmare." He whispered, his voice smooth. His eyes were full of warmth when he stared at the male. Loud Tail's tail was swaying back and forth gently, hitting the male softly when he began to speak once again. "I'm here." He murmured.

"Yeah... yeah.. I know." Racing Creek mumbled, shoving his snout into the male's paws. His ears were pressed up against his skull as his tail was tucked under his belly, hidden.

"Let me go get you some prey, so you'll feel a little bit better." Loud Tail murmured, getting up and leaving the den. His tail was swaying back and forth as he exited, tapping the male with the tip of it.

Racing Creek let out a sigh when he glanced over his shoulder to see Muddy Ears and Bumble gossiping with one and another. Everyone was enjoying their lives. Did they forget about the deaths that happened? Did they forget about that cranky storyteller and the small pup?

He shook his head softly when Loud Tail walked back into the den with a rabbit hanging from his maw. The male dropped it on Racing Creek's paws with a smile forming on his face. "Here you go, Creek!" He barked, his tail swishing back and forth.

"Thanks.." His voice trailed off as he looked up at the male. "Do you ever think about the dogs that got killed and if there will be more? After all, the coyotes are still attacking us everyday." The male mumbled, taking a chunk out of the rabbit.

"I remember them." Loud Tail answered, his voice steady and emotionless. His tail was growing limp as he opened his maw again to speak. "I... there might be more murders..."

CHAPTER THIRTY

"You're getting really big." The male commented, a small chuckle escaping him. His tail was thudding against the dock as he looked down at the reflection of him and his mate.

Bumble furrowed her brows as she shot a glare at Rippling River. "What's that supposed to mean?" She questioned, her head tilting to the side. The female was holding onto her booby bird plush as she glared at the male, waiting for a response. It was disrespectful to call females *big* or any dog really. Even if she was expecting pups, it was rude to call her big.

Rippling River opened his maw to speak but nothing came out. "Er... well... uhm.. I didn't mean it that way. Like uhm you're beautiful." He murmured, glancing away while his pelt heated up at the embarrassment. "Sorry..." The male mumbled, dipping his maw into the water, his spine shivering at the sudden coldness that had shot through his leg.

She leaned against him and licked his cheek. "It's fine." The female murmured, her voice sweeter than apple pie. Her tail was swaying back and forth as she tried to think of something to call him. "You look quite dapper yourself today."

"Thank you." He barked, his head dipping down while his nose touched the freeing water. His tail was swishing back and forth as he wiggled his haunches. He was a water dog. He was born to swim. A smirk crawled onto his face and he splashed down into the water.

Water droplets got thrown up into the air and hit Bumble in the face. She scoffed as she gazed down at him, her brow furrowing at the male. "Are you really in that water?" She questioned, her head tilting to the side as she watched the male.

"Yeah! It's what I'm meant to do!" He barked, slapping the water with his front paw. Droplets went flying once again and slapped the female in the chest. His tail was whacking the water back and forth while he swam in place.

She rolled her eyes. "Hit me again with that water and we'll see who steals your favorite piece of prey from the prey pile." Bumble chuckled, watching him swim around with joy swarming around his dark colored eyes.

Snarls began to erupt from the shadows. A dog crawled out of the shadows with a wicked smirk placed on her face. She was cackling with laughter when she approached Bumble. The female licked her chops when she curled her tail over the expecting female.

The canine's tail flicked and coyotes started to flood the place. Growls were heard and dagger sharp fangs were shown. Blood lust was swirling around their slitted eyes as they stared at Bumble but then at her mate who was slowly making his way to shore.

"Don't hurt her!" He snarled, shaking his pelt and water went flying once again. His tail was raised when he sent his sharp glare to all the coyotes who were starting to surround him yet the female was near Bumble holding her paw against her neck. None of the coyotes went over to her.

"Oh we won't, darling." She purred, scraping Bumble's chin with her nails. "Oh wait oops, didn't mean to dig my nails into her chin." The female chuckled, holding the struggling female down with her paws. She whipped her head to the side, her pointed ears pressing up against her skull. "Kill him."

"Don't!" Bumble cried, struggling under the female's grasp.

The coyotes swarmed the male, biting his legs and snout. At least two of them had their fangs hooked onto his throat. Within minutes the male dropped dead and the coyotes scattered, never to be seen again. Eyes wide open with terror while blood was splattered over his body.

"We will do more for this territory." The multi-colored

female purred, letting go of Bumble and starting to back up into the shadows.

"I will fight for this territory even if it's not mine. I don't care if blood is thrown around. I will fight to honor him. I will fight." Bumble cried, tears soaking her cheeks. "I'll fight!" She cried again.

Made in the USA
Coppell, TX
01 May 2021

54873004R00098